IMPRINT

A collection of short stories and
poems exploring identity.

Imprint

A Bournemouth Writing Prize Anthology

First published 2022 by Fresher Publishing

Fresher Publishing
Bournemouth University
Weymouth House
Fern Barrow
Poole
Dorset BH12 5BB

www.fresherpublishing.co.uk

email: bournemouthwritingprize@bournemouth.ac.uk

Lead cover designer: Lucy Pearce
Assistant designers: Rosie Clayton, Sonika Karjinni and Milie Fiirgaard

Foreword

Our identities are as unique as fingerprints. They can be found within us through our cultures, beliefs, appearances and much more - and they can inspire great art.

For this collection, we chose to highlight the way in which women view this complex subject and have selected short stories and poems in which you might find yourself, lose yourself and find yourself again.

Be it an exploration of sexuality or motherhood, grief or love, there's a moment for everyone in *Imprint*. The pages offer a myriad of thoughts and experiences to reflect on and, even though this anthology is written entirely by women, we believe it will be read and enjoyed by all.

The featured pieces were carefully selected from the many submissions to the Bournemouth Writing Prize, and some of which were shortlisted. As MA Creative Writing and Publishing students at Bournemouth University, we had the pleasure of reading and editing these pieces. We hope you enjoy them as much as we have.

From Lucy, Milie, Rosie and Sonika
Welcome to *Imprint*

Contents

Mixology
Sue Finlay

(Extracts from: A Guide to Life's Cocktails)

Dad's Fruit Punch@The Willows, Alconberry Weston
If you are drinking Dad's Fruit Punch, make sure that no one at the party sees you. It will be in a huge, silver-plated tureen with six lion heads embossed around the side. The colour of the punch won't match any of the colouring pencils in your Bumper 100 Crayola Set and your big brother, Steve, will have told you that it smells like Mr Brady's chemistry lab. There will be pieces of apple and slices of orange sloshing around in it. Dad will be using a silver ladle to serve it into cut glass tumblers and handing it out to the guests as they arrive. Mum will be wearing a sparkly trouser suit and will be wandering round the guests with a plate of vol-au-vents. You will be in red ladybird pyjamas from Woolworths. Briefly wonder if Steve has noticed his favorite Scooby Doo pencil topper is missing as you squeeze it in your pocket.

When Dad leaves the fruit punch station to talk to Phil from Business Studies, sidle over and pretend to stir it, but ladle some into Steve's Scooby Doo mug. When you look up, Varsha from Legal will be watching you, but she'll wink. Decide to be like Varsha when you grow up. Put a couple of sausage rolls and cocktail stick skewers in your pocket and make for the stairs, where Steve will be waiting. Take a quick slug from the Scooby Doo mug before you hand it over to him. While you are coughing, he will have downed it in a oner. He'll stand up and beat his chest with his fists and say 'scooby dooby doo' in a silly voice that makes you laugh.

Sit on the stairs and eat the sausage rolls and cocktail stick skewers. When you have finished, Steve will stand up and try to fart in your face and you will scream. He'll put you in a headlock. Stab him in the leg with the cocktail stick.

Brandy and Babycham@Student Union bar, Freshers Week

If you have ordered Brandy and Babycham, make sure it's your fifth one before loudly exclaiming that alcohol doesn't really affect you that much and you can drink literally gallons before feeling anything. Laugh like a hyena at Benji's joke about his parents dropping him off and his mum crying. When Golden Brown comes on the jukebox, pretend to know all the lyrics and tell everyone you've seen The Stranglers live *at least* ten times.

Drink three more Brandy and Babychams before falling into the arms of Reagan, who will drag you off to the loos. While you are being sick, listen to her telling you she fancies Mike. Don't tell her you fancy him too. Never tell her. Stagger back to the bar arm in arm and announce that there's a party round your place tonight. Crowd into the off-licence at the end of your road, then pile into the Chippie next door for bags of steaming hot chips. Burn the roof of your mouth off eating them too quickly.

Watch Benji run up the middle of the road towards you wearing a traffic cone on his head, his arms outstretched. Feel alive. Feel free.

Bellinis@The Big Party Barn, Cotswolds

If you are drinking Bellinis at Reagan's Hen Party Weekend, you will be using penis straws to drink them.

You will be sitting in a hot tub wearing pink fluffy Deely boppers that say 'head bridesmaid'. Also in the hot tub will be Phoebe, Emily and Chloe from uni, Esther, Becka, Ruby and Ems from home, Reagan's mum, and someone called Pam.

After a while, no one will bother making Bellinis, they'll just pour prosecco straight into random tumblers they've found in the cupboards. Pam won't even bother with the tumbler. Later on, when it gets to playing Mr and Mrs, Reagan's mum will take over. She'll have been emailing Mike questions for the past two weeks. Laugh with everyone else when Reagan gets an answer wrong, even though you know the right answer.

Slip outside for some fresh air. Walk to the end of the garden. Pam will be there smoking and she'll offer you a cigarette. Take it. Inhale deeply and hold the smoke in your lungs before letting it drift lazily out of your mouth. Don't think about any of it, just let the nicotine do its work.

Sex on the Beach@All-inclusive, Jamaica

If you have ordered Sex on the Beach, make sure you drink it in the Caribbean, sitting on a stool at a bar that has a fringe of dried palms. There will be a coating of sand on your ankles, like sugar on shortbread.

When the bartender places the cocktail in front of you, don't ask him if he used premium spirits to make it. He will have a white gash of a smile that cuts through his tan and eyes that read you like a high-end magazine, flicking through, casually.

Part your salt-dried lips, place them around the straw, then turn away. Don't think about your divorce or what your mum said. Draw deeply. Put on your aviators. Let your sarong drift down from your right shoulder. Wave to Mike and Reagan as they walk hand in hand along the shoreline.

Try not to swallow, just let it slide down your throat. Enjoy the coldness then the warmth as it enters your brain. Sigh.

When you get to the end, don't suck the dregs, leave them. Turn back to the bartender. He will be leaning at the other end of the bar, waiting. You won't have to say a thing.

Raspberry Crush@The Vicarage, St Nicholas Parish Church

If you are drinking a Raspberry Crush, it will be because you are standing in the garden of the Vicarage after the christening of Zephie Aura.

You will be making polite conversation with the vicar. Zephie will be sleeping blissfully in your arms, having screamed blue murder in the church only ten minutes ago. She will be wearing white socks and a floral print dress edged with lace. One of the socks will be dangling, half off, waiting to fall. The vicar will be enquiring politely about your religious qualifications to be a godmother. Deflect by smiling and lying about all the charities you support. When you look up, Mike will be watching you. Look away.

Reagan will come up from behind and encircle you and Zephie in her arms. She will very subtly whisper something naughty about the vicar while pretending to tuck your hair behind your ear. Clamp your lips tight shut so as not to laugh. You will hear a distant hum of insects as they buzz around the buffet.

Zephie will stir dreamily in your arms, her lips making a tiny 'o' shape. Stroke her cheek with your finger. Mike will walk across the lawn and take her from you, gently, without waking her, and kiss her forehead. Feel lost. Feel alone.

Gin and Tonic@The Ivy, West Street, London

If you are drinking a Gin and Tonic at The Ivy, the

bartender will ask you what gin you want. He will hand you a menu and wait. Turn the pages as though you know what you are looking for, then point at one. He will nod sagely and spend a long time on it. He will present it to you in an overlarge glass bowl on a long stem, with ribbons of shaved cucumber and two or three black peppercorns floating around the surface.

Take it to a corner table where you can watch people. Try to ignore the middle-aged lady sitting on her own. She will be waving her arms around and talking about how no one knows how to make a proper gin and tonic these days. She might be talking to you, but you can't be sure. Nod, but don't meet her eye.

Look at your phone and check that this was the right venue and the right time. Sip slowly. Don't be tipsy, just relaxed. When Arlo enters, check your phone to see if his photo matches his profile picture. Watch him closely as he goes to the bar and orders a drink. Don't introduce yourself until you have decided if he is okay or not. Decide what okay means at this point in your life. When you are satisfied that he is acceptable, leave the table and go over. He will be quietly spoken, attentive, and he will make you laugh. Allow yourself to be charmed. When he asks if you'd like another drink, don't hesitate. Say yes.

Warm oat milk with a dash of whisky@St Luke's Hospice
If you are drinking warm oat milk, make sure you take a hip flask of whisky to add to it, hidden in your handbag. Before you enter the building, steel yourself. Mike and Zephie will be in the cafe downstairs and will leap up when they see you. You will all hug and try not to cry. They will fill you in on how things are. You will go up to Reagan's room and walk up and down for ten minutes, taking deep breaths, before you go in.

Reagan will do her best attempt at a smile. There will be oxygen tubes sticking out of her nose and a canister sitting at her side. The suck and draw will be a musical backdrop as you sit on her bed. Make her laugh by likening the sound to the sucking of Bellinis through a penis straw. Lay your head in her lap. She will stroke your hair. Tell her you love her. Tell her what she means to you. Don't cry. She will say that she is sorry about Mike, that she knew all along how you felt. Say no. Say it doesn't matter.

When the nurse comes in with warmed oat milk, wait for her to leave before taking the hip flask out of your bag. Slosh it in. Hold the cup to her mouth and let her take a sip, before taking a slug yourself from the same cup. She will try to make a joke about it tasting like Brandy and Babycham, before falling asleep. Tiptoe out. Shut the door quietly so as not to wake her.

Champagne and canapes@Edinburgh University

If you are drinking Champagne and eating canopes, make sure you are standing in a white marquee in the grounds of the McEwan Hall. The sides of the marquee will be flapping about, angrily. You will be wearing a summer dress but wishing you hadn't.

Zephie will be wearing a black gown and mortar board. She will be high, ecstatic, joyous. Her friends will be the same. They will be laughing and hugging and taking group pictures and selfies. There will be no end to their delight. Parents and family will be cradling drinks and stuffing canopes into their mouths, watching on. Zephie will throw her arms around you and thank you for coming. She will drag you off to meet Lissie, Ava, Isabel, Calum and Luke. They will say 'Hi' and talk politely to you for a few minutes. Move away. Let them get on with it.

Stand next to Mike and chink glasses. Don't say you

must be so proud. Wait for him to speak. Look at his grey hair and his slight stoop. He will produce a black and white photograph of your graduation. Fish your reading glasses out of your bag. Look at it and say, 'look at us'. He will ask if you remember that night, after Reagan had gone to bed. Take the photograph from him and stare at Reagan. She will be smiling directly at the camera, jubilant, happy. You and Mike will be turned towards her. Say gosh what a long time ago.

After you hand the photograph back, tell him you must go, you have a plane to catch. Hug him tightly. Feel his skin on your skin. Smell his aftershave. Wave goodbye to Zephie. Walk away.

The McCallum Chin

Sharon Black

Protruding, almost petulant, this chin
runs through the women of our bloodline

like a rhizome, sprouting its potato
through the pale soil

of our Ayrshire faces. These chins
don't quiver, dimple, or itch to fight:

they're unassuming all their lives
then jut, spectacular, above an ageing neck.

There's Grandma Roberts in her housecoat,
a tuft of wiry hairs on hers;

Gran, all flowery plates and fruitcake slices,
under hers two loops of pearls;

Mum, buttoned up, heading for the leisure club,
hers shiny from Olay. And mine,

one in a queue stretching across the generations –
deceased, alive, and waiting to be born –

bobbing up the line, waggling
at the family gossip, stepping forward

when our names are called, rising briefly into view

then out again, making babies,

getting jobs, falling ill,
burying our dead,

doing our best to take it on our chins,
doing our best to keep them up.

Dotted Line

Milie Fiirgaard Rasmussen

A thought popped into my head that night
    when you were drunk, throwing up
        and having a fight with yourself.
That's all well and good – True,
    but then the thought that I kinda wanted to
        kiss you?

I'm blaming the wine,
    as you drunkenly attempt to make the
    bathroom wall re   cline
        like an airplane seat –
        you complain about heat
        on your cheek,
    as I remove the dirty socks from your feet.

There's a time and a place –
    I've got impulse control, although,
I'm sure that my face would
give a peek of my soul –

If we weren't so drunk... My braid has come undone.

I stare at your hair –
    it's so long, it's so lush,
    I swear it's the alcohol making me blush.
        Your hair really is pretty –
        all the curls down your back –
            right where your bra's about ready

to snap...

Wait, no! I mean, it's just cute,
looks fab – Shit.

I think the Somersby was heavenly –
        it messed up my mind though.
Thoughts like these are endless;
        it's quite easy to find yourself
                caught up in a moment –
                        you know what I mean?
        It's a side of myself, I hadn't yet seen.

You know..? I hope –
Or, nevermind – it's a joke
how I can't distinguish a relation;
        I have a very shaky foundation.
        It should be straight forward, a straight line,
                straight ahead
        but you're a dot in this spot –
                Maybe I misread myself?

I don't actually know where I'm going with this –
I digress, it's just stress, probably?
I should really just talk less.

Ragdoll
Aisling Watters

When she looked in the paper cup, there was no coffee in it;
she never pressed the button. The guy beside her wearing
a Stetson (that was the kind of place she lived in) saw her
noticing this, so she told him – as though to reassure him
of her faculties – that she never pressed the button, and
then made a *pfft* noise, spraying spit in the narrow space
between them. The guy smiled and left his station with his
cup of coffee in his large calloused hand. Most of the men
around there had large calloused hands. She turned to the
machine again and pressed the button – hard, thinking
about how there had been something about his smile. It
was the smile you give to a loose woman. A smile that was
almost a smirk. And she found that she did not have the
will to be offended, feeling as loose as she felt. Velvety,
almost.

She'd decided to get drunk at lunch. Well, it wasn't so
much a decision, more an incremental process, which she'd
hardly been involved in. Like a patron who shows up to cut
the ribbon of an exhibition. They'd been at the restaurant
across the road from the petrol station and really, it had
been the toilet roll's fault. It had always been white but
for some reason, the toilet roll in the one restaurant in the
tiny Midwest town that she had settled in with her college
boyfriend, was peach. Yes. Peach. Or maybe apricot. One of
the fruits. And as much as she tried, her sphincter refused
to release any urine, knowing the peach massacre that
would leave the area dry but traumatised. Perhaps that
sounded dramatic. But she had a long history with peach
toilet roll. Growing up, her father wouldn't let any other
shade of toilet roll into the house, and the one time her

mother came home with a pack of white, he deliberately broke the fuse box, so they were out of electricity for weeks until his frustration and apathy (he never stopped to think about the TV) took precedence over all other emotions and he fixed it. Still, the whole experience had been enough for her mother – or more so her and her siblings who usually did the weekly shop – to know that there was to only ever be one shade of toilet roll in the house: peach.

Once she started thinking about toilet roll, she thought about other things, and like those connect-the-dot pictures her sons never liked, it all became too much, and she found herself drinking enough glasses of wine that it felt as though the restaurant was encased in honey or marzipan or something turgid and sticky. But she was aware that she'd spilled things; she couldn't read the dessert menu without squinting; her husband had taken care of their three boys the entire time, and between cleaning faces and wiping spills, he had barely touched his dinner.

It was the toilet roll's fault.

The sound of pouring coffee was exaggerating what was already her pressing need to pee. But it seemed like too mammoth of a task to purchase a coffee and use the petrol station's toilet, so she looked around for distraction and there, right beside the coffee station, was a stand dedicated to St. Patrick's Day paraphernalia – or a glut of green crap that most likely wouldn't sell because there was talk of the parades being cancelled due to the virus spreading across countries like a dangerous zephyr. And with that thought rooted firmly at the back of her mind, she had to accede that the stand was comforting in a way; like a raft offering some safety in a sea of uncertainty. So she inspected what was on the stand, discerning shapes that became items that generally fell into a mawkish or cute category. Well, there was only one thing cute. A ragdoll. She picked it up and laughed at the tag bearing an image of a lecherous leprechaun and the inevitable strip of paper attached to its bottom that had the words *MADE IN CHINA* written on it, and beneath this, a row of symbols denoting whether the ragdoll could be washed and dried.

The tumble dryer was her favourite household appliance. Expensive, yes, but she didn't have to worry about that seeing as she hadn't worked since the birth of her firstborn. A few months before, on a day that was not particularly different to any other day, she decided to put some washed clothes into the dryer even though it was a bright breezy day. Because once she put the clothes in the dryer, she could forget about them, whereas in addition to the effort of hanging them on the washing line, she might have to dash back out to retrieve them if it rained. There was a part of her, a small part, that knew it was wasteful and indolent, so she put the laundry basket back on the kitchen table and sat beside her eldest who had just walked home from school and was eating a slice of bread layered in Nutella (she had no idea where her two youngest were – hopefully in the playpen in the sitting room).

'They're in their beds,' said her eldest. 'I gave them juice and closed the safety gate on the stairs.'

He was such a good boy, her eldest. Even with chocolate daubing his round cheeks, you could still tell he was a good boy. Too good. It was like he wanted his goodness to outweigh their positions. Except it was more than that; he was like a little tyrant waiting for any moment to pull rank. She was the mother. He was the child. Too often, he forgot this, and so, she found herself leaning towards him, leaning further when he edged away, keeping his eyes on the table – *her* eyes – wasted on his father's plain face.

'Never forget that you're the reason I drink.'

His expression remained neutral, but she saw his

half-eaten slice of bread lower in his hand, and then, in a movement so quick for someone who prided herself on minimum effort, she smacked it to the ground.

'Eat it!'

He looked at her. Pain swimming in the eyes that he'd stolen from her. And with this pain, she knew she had him. He never could evade her grasp like his younger siblings who, as well as being flanked by his protection, had that innate younger sibling trait of repudiation; already, she knew that she would never ask them to eat bread off the floor. But her eldest would always be refused the luxury of exception, and as she stood over him, watching him eat the bread off the floor, she poured the wet basket of laundry over his head.

'When you're done, put those in the dryer.'

It was her eldest's fault. He did it to spite her. Such a good, deserving boy, who knew all about child locks and safety gates and regularly held his mother's hair back while she vomited into the kitchen sink and never failed to ask her each morning what he could do today to make her life better; knew that clothes shouldn't be in the tumble dryer for hours on end and that his little brother's Halloween Batman costume and his other little brother's Halloween Spiderman costume both might be flammable.

Later, she would think that she shouldn't have asked him to eat the bread off the floor. But it was still his fault. Although she was grateful that he carried his two little brothers to safety and dragged her to the front lawn, where she woke to her husband screaming in her face. She had never seen him so mad. Someone less numb would have been frightened. She knew he wouldn't have screamed if she hadn't been so wasted. No. If the same situation occurred and she had been sober, he would have embraced her and their three perfect children in front of their dream home, creaking and crackling from the strain of the blaze that was so powerful its smoke airbrushed out the stars. But nothing like this happened; he just kept screaming at her until his eyes bulged and a vein in his short, reliable neck throbbed. She found herself wanting to volunteer to be hit just to get it out of him: this stark rage that was everything he was not, but she was.

It was like they swapped places that night. But he didn't hit her. And she never did offer herself as bait, but just stood there, hiding behind her hair, only realising when he stopped screaming that she was in her underwear and a vest. Both her jeans and jumper had been pulled off her in her eldest's efforts to remove her from the house. She looked at him, his hair sticking out at all sorts of angles, soot covering his cheeks where, hours before, there had been chocolate, and his boy's arms hanging by his side, depleted of all strength after saving each member of his family who had been in the house. An unsung hero, which, believe it or not, she had once been herself; the kid who would fold themself up or turn into whatever shape necessary if it meant that somebody else's needs were met first.

'Come here,' she said, and her eldest came to her, as she knew he would, and his younger siblings followed, as she knew they would. Then their father wrapped his arms around them as she couldn't be certain he would.

It was her fault.

Deep down, she knew this, and so, for months, she was good. So good it hurt. Like smiling too hard or helping someone you loathe. For months, she was that person. It is exhausting, being good. Nobody ever tells you this. Especially not the good. And then it came, as she knew it would: the bad. Crawling like a spider up a drain, all limbs and incorrigible will. It manifested as it historically always had – through restlessness. It was like there was this internal frenzy that only those with a trained eye could perceive. Ten years of marriage and too many ructious years of dating had taught her husband to have a trained eye. No longer did she approach the refurbishment of their house with an almost drugged equanimity. No longer did she fold things corner to corner. No longer did she cook scrambled eggs or pancakes for breakfast. No longer did she kiss him goodbye and tell him to have a good day in the mornings. After so many heady magical months, the mask was not so much slipping but cracking, leaving particles of clay stippled across floorboards, the front lawn, the interior of their car, the local supermarket, church, football pitch, school.

Not much mask remained. Sensing this, her husband suggested that they go out for lunch that Sunday to the local restaurant, which was not very romantic but 'family-friendly'. He'd looked at her when he said it – imploring her to remember that she was part of a unit now. As though she could forget. But to her credit, she made an extra effort with her outfit and listened to her husband as he recited the menu they knew off by heart. And after they gave their orders to the young waitress, who kept smiling at them as though they were something pinned to her vision board, her husband gazed adoringly at their children, winking at the eldest who'd been beaming for months, and then at her, mesmerised, like she was a supernova or some sort of phenomenon.

And in ways, she was.

'Wait,' she said, clutching the waitress's apron. Looking at her, she could see the girl's vision board smouldering in her eyes. Meanwhile, the rest of her mask slid to the floor. 'Can I get a glass of red?'

She managed to pour some milk into the coffee, but the

task of the lid was not so seamless. She disposed of two lids before finally jamming one on, knowing, as she held it, that it was not secured properly as she could feel rivulets of coffee on the top of her hand, not scalding her as they should.

Once again, she was numb. Gloriously numb.

In the hand not holding the cup of coffee was the ragdoll. Having three boys meant that she'd never had a reason to hold a toy that held so much finesse. The green dress, all tulle and frills, was not entirely unlike her wedding dress. She'd deliberately opted for over the top, thinking that if people were distracted by her dress then they wouldn't notice how drunk she was, which turned out to be true up until the moment she walked into a door and smashed her nose. And apart from the fact that it was wool and three different shades of green, her hair had been the same as the ragdoll's on her wedding day; scooped up into ribbons and flowing at the back. And she'd also had long (false) eyelashes, fluttering them all day at guests, hoping her eyes were iridescent and wifely, but not too wifely, and lined plum lips – but unlike the ragdoll, she did not have a shamrock sewn onto her face beneath one of her perfect dry eyes.

She thought the shamrock was like those fake beauty spots that old Hollywood movie stars used to paint on their cheekbones like a stamp to further prove their gross value. All these details for a small, inexpensive ragdoll, and yet, if you looked closer, you could see that she was barely held together with coarse stitching around her jaw and hairline: the ears looked particularly painful. And not only had the designers not bothered to give her some sort of pudendum, but they'd given her these oven glove hands whereby her fingers were fused together. But despite these glaring oversights, they had made sure that she was beautiful and to sew a Shamrock onto her face; to provide a stamp to prove her worth.

She was outraged. So outraged, she slammed the money on the cash desk and left the coffee that had been such an effort to make, ignoring the shop assistant calling after her, nearly walking into the automatic doors, and settling back into the passenger seat of the car. She no longer cared so much about the silence of her three boys or her husband's vice grip of the steering wheel because she had problems of her own.

Her ragdoll was syndactyl.

'Where's your coffee?'

'What coffee?'

'You said you were going in there to get coffee.'

'I forgot it.'

She'd had a ragdoll as a child. She used to play with it in the shed. They'd pretend to have tea parties over the lawnmower and empty cans of petrol and diaphanous spiderwebs and one rusted bike that only the older kids reaped the benefits of. And it was there that one day she stood, holding her ragdoll, watching her father's body swing from a rope tied to a beam, a step ladder lying on the ground.

After what felt like weeks of frenzy, of unwanted Pyrex dishes (never again would she eat lasagna or casseroles), of chilling Mass cards and limp bouquets, she walked out of the house, away from her mother's tears and her siblings' sighs, and tied her ragdoll to a bough she could reach on the only tree in the street. Each day, she would look out the window of her shared bedroom to see if it was still there, hanging by its yellow hair, its gingham dirndl getting dirtier by the hour, and each day its inexplicable resistance caused a node of fury in her chest. Until one day, she looked out and the ragdoll was gone; snatched by a raven, stolen by a child with even fewer toys than she had or stuck on some part of a haulage truck seeing the sights of Europe for free. What surprised her most was how dismayed she felt, like she had burst a blister only to have to begin the healing process all over again.

The news was on in the background. She tried not to listen to it as she sat on the couch, holding the ragdoll inches away from her face, and it arrived, as she knew it would; the voice that occurred at certain moments in her life, most recently after the birth of her last child.

Go die.

'No,' she said, squeezing the ragdoll, embedding her thumbs into its face until its features distorted. But the voice continued to rise, even after she shoved it under a cushion; cresting so high that she couldn't understand how the paint was not peeling from the walls, how the windows did not shatter or the roof fall in. Louder and louder it became, until she couldn't understand why her husband was not rushing into the sitting room, why the dogs in the street were not howling, the sirens of police cars blaring, until the only conclusion she could reach was: it was coming from her.

She dashed out of the house, knowing from experience that motion was the only force to match the sound, so she did not stop running until she reached the lamp post at the end of the street and tied the ragdoll to it, running away without glancing back, relieved that the voice was gone by the time she reached the house. As soon as her breathing steadied, she went into the sitting room to join her husband, waiting for her on the couch as she knew he would be, ready to speak to her at length about rehab, but then they were distracted from themselves by the news, by the virus rapidly sweeping through terrains, making its way towards them and everyone else. They braced themselves.

Ragdoll

Dainty

Faith McNamara

I've always wanted to be smaller
To take up less space
Fall below prying eyes
No longer be right there, in your face

My limbs to be wiry thin
Like that in a flower found
Constantly wrestled by the winds
But always rooted to the ground

Oh, to be seen as a fragile bird
Something to be clutched at and held
Clasped in strong, weathered hands
Hand fed ideas to believe in and beheld

But I am not these things
I am large and loud
Screaming out my thoughts
Always standing out in a crowd

Though I've always wanted to be smaller
Maybe it's okay to occupy this space

Buttoning Ailsa's Coat

Maureen Cullen

Mum finished a row, wrapped her needles in the half-formed sleeve and announced she had a job for me, informing me of the task wi her usual barked out matter-of-factness. No thought was given tae the effect on my tender mind or tae my digestion, stretched out as I was across the couch after my big tea of sausage and chips.

I sat up and whined. 'How come Aunty Betty wasnae chosen?'

Mum tucked her knitting behind a cushion and stood up. 'Yer Aunt Betty's lily-livered and wouldnae cope.'

I wanted tae shout out that I was only thirteen and couldnae cope. But saying that aloud would get me a skite. It wasnae fair.

Mum merely patted me on the shoulder before taking off her glasses and wiping them on her sleeve. Her sea-green eyes became their normal size but magnified again on return of the specs. Fine spidery lines radiated from under the rims. I hadnae noticed that before. She turned and took the purse out of her pinny pocket and placed three shillings on the mantelpiece.

'For the metre, hen.'

I followed her movements open-mouthed, willing her tae change her mind, but she nodded tae the weans, took her coat and bag from the press, and left for her cleaning job as usual.

I looked for comfort from Marie, the only sibling who could string two words thegither. She sat perched on the armchair, ears trained tae the lobby and stairs. Ailsa leaned in tight against her big sister, thumb in gob, snot running from her nose. Wee Callum stayed fast asleep, his stripy-blue chest rising and falling in his new second-hand pram. When the front door clicked shut, Marie, ay cautious that Mum could be in two places at once, piped up at last.

'Jings, Annette, glad it's you and no me.' She waltzed both eyes around her heid.

'Your time will come, believe you me,' I said.

'Don't think so. This is a one and only.' She scratched her bum.

Saturday finally arrived after three nights of the same weird dream where I was being chased by a three-heided nun wi a giant drill. On waking, I identified the heids as sisters Marie-Claire, Angelique and Jean-Paul, aw three as gleeful at my failure as a fugitive as they were daily at my pains as a pupil. I woke each night in a sweat, disturbing Ailsa who howled at the darkness and only settled back tae sleep wi the ceiling light on, which alerted Marie and her girnin gob. Having tae share my very bed wi these two at the age of thirteen was just another catastrophe.

Any other Saturday morning, I'd have been eager tae escape the house, but not today. The bus let us off in the deserted square under the town clock at ten tae nine. It was a ghostly scene wi frost whitened roofs, powdered pavements, and drooping fir trees lining the church graveyard. My fingers yearned for the cheer of the red double-decker as it rumbled away round the corner. I could easily sprint after it, catch the bar, and haul myself aboard. Being in the first 11 at school, on right wing, I was a force tae be reckoned wi. The sisters never got tae witness my prowess as an athlete; they couldnae even climb the hill tae the sports fields, so weighed down were they by blubber. I sighed and stepped the other way, catching up wi Mum as she picked her way ower cobbles. She hadnae spoken a word since we'd left the house. Aunty Betty had arrived just in time tae watch the weans, chain smoking as usual.

When I pleaded wi her tae take my place, she blew a smoke ring in my face and said, 'no on yer nelly, hen.'

The mouth of the close loomed and Mum stepped in first, disappearing intae the gloom, her footsteps echoing back through the building. I followed her up the winding stairs, gripping the banister tae steady myself. On the first landing, a huge stained-glass window dazzled my eyes. It was as if someone had thrown a bucket of stars at the jewelled panes, they so shimmered wi frost. Even if it meant freezing tae death, I'd have gladly sat for the rest of the day on the step under that window.

We climbed the second flight tae the next floor where yellow lamps barely lit up chequered linoleum. Only one door stood on the landing; a sign hanging inside its window said *Open*. Bunching my fists, I stepped back while Mum turned the knob. It rattled, but the door creaked ajar.

'Come on,' she said, frowning. We entered a reception hall decorated wi brass pots holding green rubber plants. A horrid whiff of antiseptic hit me.

'Wait here,' Mum said.

I stood quivering as she spoke tae the receptionist. The woman, smartly dressed in a beige polo-neck and a green checked skirt, stepped out from behind her desk and gestured Mum through a door. I stared after the woman's trim waist and hips, noting the confident tilt of her chin and wondered how you got a job as a receptionist. Probably needed Highers for that; being good at hockey wouldnae swing it. There wasnae a Higher in anything I was good at, like watching weans, changing nappies and frying chips. The woman was holding the door open for me so I skittered through.

The waiting room was empty. More brass pots wi

collapsed plants stood on a cracked tiled floor. A scratched table stacked wi tattered magazines took up most of the space. A jumble of odd dining chairs stood against three walls. As we sat down, I tuned intae sounds coming from somewhere close. Drilling, suction, metal clanging on metal. My stomach see-sawed, my mouth filled wi sourness. I gagged, but held it down.

'Mum, I don't feel well.'

There was a chance I might be let off if I were sick, but when she replied, 'me as well, hen,' I knew it was hopeless. She peeked out from behind her glasses wi a look so lost, so desperate, that I forgot my aches. Aw that had happened in the past three months was nothing tae this. My mother was never lost, never desperate. Even when she'd found out about Da's shenanigans, she hadnae folded. Out he went, bags at his arse. Drinking and fighting were bad enough, but the bit o stuff was the last straw. I'd been so excited when I came home from school that day tae.

'Yer da's oot the hoose and he's never coming back.' The very house expanded wi relief.

I shimmied closer and laced my arm through hers, feeling the rise and fall of her chest through our coats. The hospital said she must have aw her teeth extracted, the gum disease could cause major health problems, and she was anaemic. The new baby had stolen aw her calcium. It'd have tae be false teeth when her gums healed. I shivered, but stilled myself.

'Listen, Mum.'

She turned tae me.

'It'll aw be done in a half hour. You'll get the gas, you willnae have a clue. And don't worry, I'll get you home. I've got the shillings for the taxi in my pocket.' My voice sounded squeaky.

'Aye, hen. Course, it'll be fine. Yer a guid girl. Go tae the toilet if ye like.'

'No, it's awright, it's calmed a bit.' I clutched my tummy.

The window had clear panes wi *Havoc Town Dentist* printed across in frosted lettering, reversed but readable from inside. I wondered about the folly of advertising such a place. My mind dashed out nonsense: dental havoc, havoc of dentistry, havoc tae aw who come here. 'Gie's yer teeth!' I nearly giggled. Stamping that down, something else rose from deep inside and I itched tae thump that glass. But I still had my arm through Mum's. Maybe I should've been more helpful tae her in the last few weeks. In my mind, her competence and strictness were both intertwined, like the roots of the magnolia bush in the school rotunda, the one next tae the Virgin Mary. Mum never had time for self-pity and went about her business wi stoic determination.

Folk's voices carried up from the street. Shopfront grilles were being unhinged for the day, a car tooted, a boat on the Clyde shrilled its horn. But it aw seemed so far away from us here. It occurred tae me that Mum and I were never alone thegither; we ay had the weans about us or she was at work or I was at school.

'The wireless weatherman thinks it might snow.' Mum shivered, though it was warm in the waiting room.

I hugged her tighter, her wool coat chafing my chin.

She laid her heid on my shoulder and gied a big sigh. 'Ah'm glad ah didnae huv tae come by massel.'

Shame gripped me; I'd tried my best tae get out of this, and even now sitting here, I was glad it was her and not me.

We tensed as the door opened and the receptionist announced, 'the dentist is ready for you, Mrs Crawford.'

Mum patted my knee and got up. I held back tears until the door clicked shut behind her, but soon they trickled down my cheeks unhindered, salting my lips. I clapped my hands tae my ears tae deafen whooshing sounds, metal pinging, and ding after ding, which I imagined were teeth dropping intae a bowl. My breath surged tae rapid gasps. Remembering my first aid class, I put my heid between my knees. It helped, and once I had my breathing under control, I prayed. First the Our Father, then a Glory Be, and by the time I was on my hundred-and-something Hail Mary, the door opened and the receptionist came in.

'Your mum's all done now. She's recovering well, and I've telephoned for the taxi.' She must've seen the state of me because her business-like face softened. 'I'll come down the stairs and help her intae the car. Let me get my coat. But don't worry if she's talking a lot of nonsense, that's the gas. Just put her to bed for the day.'

I followed the woman through the hallway, glancing at the dental theatre as I passed. A raised seat tilted backwards beside gas canisters wi tubes and knobs, instruments of torture sat on a tall cabinet and, beside a deep white sink, the dentist – a huge hairy man wi bulging eyes – was removing a rubber face mask. The wail that rose from my belly reached my throat, but I swallowed it down.

In the anteroom, a figure was sitting on a stool wi a basin on her knee and a handful of bloodied gauze at her face. I almost didnae recognise her as she swooned and moaned, her face blanched white. Her free hand fluttered about her heid as if unattached. I tensed, fighting flight.

I turned tae the receptionist and stuttered, 'where's her glasses?'

The woman stared at me a moment, turned on her heels, and returned wi them laid across her palm. I placed them on Mum's face and she blinked her eyes half-open.

The receptionist took Mum by the elbow and teased her tae her feet. Mum's eyes rolled and I thought she'd collapse, but her helper knew her stuff, holding her in a vice grip. I hurried in and took the other arm. The receptionist threw

Mum's coat ower her shoulders and between us we cajoled her arms through the sleeves. Finally, the woman wrapped a roll of bandage around Mum's heid, pinning it at the back so it covered her ears and held a cotton pad in place at her mouth.

'Just keep this on until you get home; the bleeding will stop soon.'

'Annette,' Mum murmured, 'ma lovely girl.' She definitely wasnae herself; she was well under the effects of the gas.

I buttoned up her coat, like I did wi Ailsa, but fumbling aw the while, thrown by the strangeness of it. It felt like an intrusion. We half carried her downstairs tae the taxi at the kerb. The driver looked a bit sickly as he helped Mum in. I climbed in beside her and we drove off, the kind woman waving tae us, concern darkening her face. Mum slept during the taxi ride while I kept my gaze on the road.

At the gate, I asked the driver tae peep his horn tae alert Aunty Betty. He did so, got out, gied me a nervous smile, then helped Mum out of the car and tae the front door. Betty had come part way downstairs tae meet us but stopped mid-step as we climbed up tae our first floor flat. Instead of gathering Mum up, she dithered.

'Oh my, oh my, Jesus Christ, oh my –'

I wanted tae slap her, but she scrambled back upstairs, leaving me and the driver tae manage Mum's ascent between us.

At the top, the weans crowded the lobby. Marie's mouth opened and closed like a fish, and wee Ailsa burst out greetin when Mum swooned against the bedroom door. Betty shepherded them intae the kitchen.

I reached in my pocket for the shillings but the driver waved them away.

'Naw, it's awright, hen. Yer mam wis a guid pal tae ma

mam when she wisnae well. God bless her. Ye awright?'

'Aye, thank you.' I didnae know my mum had pals.

He hurried out, the door slamming, leaving me alone
wi Mum, whose bandage had slipped. She smiled at me
fondly, her mouth a beetroot hole. My mum's teeth hadnae
been pearly white for a long time, but this gummy, bloodied
vision made me cuff my fists tae my cheeks. I closed my
eyes, took a deep breath, and took a firm hold of my gas-
drunk mother, guiding her intae the bedroom and down on
the bed. I unbuttoned her coat – jings, I'd done the buttons
up squinty – pulled it off, unpinned the bandage and pad,
and slipped off her glasses. I placed them on the bedside
table, sat beside her and stroked her back.

She said, 'he willnae love me noo, will he?'

'Who cares,' I said wi immediate understanding now
that I was a hundred years auld, 'That bastard can rot.' If
my mum being toothless meant he wouldnae show his face
again, I was thankful.

'Aye, he is that, a bad bastard. He tellt me ah was an ugly
cow. Well, noo ah really am.' She cackled.

My spine contracted. 'No, Mum, once you get your new
teeth, you'll be hunky-dory.'

She fell back against the pillow, eyes fluttering, her
open mouth red raw, cheeks deflated like thumbed dough.
I raised her legs ontae the bed and covered her wi the
candlewick.

Tears blinded me as I felt my way tae the toilet. Once
there, I blotted my eyes wi tissue and wet a clean towel wi
hot water from the geyser. I went back tae Mum and wiped
the blood and spew from her face and throat. She was
already asleep.

I crept out of the door, closed it behind me and made my
way tae the living room where I dismissed the useless Betty,
and sat down wi the weans, Callum on my knee. Ailsa's

hair was out of its ribbons and sticking out in clumps. Dark circles of orange juice spotted the carpet, and ash had spilled out of the empty fireplace ontae the tiles. Clothes lay ower the chairs, books and jigsaws littered the floor, and Callum fair stank. When had aw this happened? Mum kept the place like a new pin. She was a cleaning enthusiast. Or at least, she used tae be.

'Listen girls, things are going tae change around here. D'ye hear me?'

'Aye, Annette.' Marie stared at me between narrowed eyes.

Ailsa stuck her thumb in her gob.

I sat up straight. 'Marie, the nappy bag. Now.'

Buttoning Ailsa's Coat

On Kerrera Island

Sharon Black

This morning, I'm hiking

in the hills of Andalusia, figs dripping
from the trees,

pomegranates splitting on hot limestone rocks
amid the scrub, miles from any road.

I'm striding, dusty,

beside a *Nationale*
somewhere in the *Midi*, my hitching thumb
hooked firmly round my rucksack strap.

I've dropped behind my friends
on Rannoch Moor, damp from sweat
and midge spray, ten miles in,

another six to reach our lodge
along the Way
that keeps dipping, re-emerging.

I'm everywhere I've ever
walked alone, exhausted, aching
with some twinge or injury

and nothing but to keep on walking,
until the rawness sings
more softly, each moment passing

to the next as the spirit disengages
from its capable machine,
pulse playing out

against a drop that could be anywhere,
each step any step, no difference
between a footfall and a life.

From Tenerife with Love

Aby Atilol

The hair that once ran past her shoulders, the envy of all the girls in her age group, lies in a clay pot in the corner of the room. Chiamanda had lost count of the number of times Ada had nicked her scalp with the blade.

'Bring it nearer,' Ada motions to the young girl holding the lamp. Another girl surveys the mud floor and picks up the hair that falls like the dark clouds at their feet.

'I still can't see,' Ada says, tilting Chiamanda's head up and down.

'Tomorrow, we do the rest.'

Ada lets her breath out, she had been holding it all through the cutting, as if breathing would slow her down. She hands Chiamanda a tub of coconut oil and a piece of the mirror she had tucked into her wrapper.

'*Ndo* – sorry, my sister. You know this is the way of our people. Your husband's death is a shock to the whole village, may his soul rest in peace.'

She takes a step back, hands on hips, satisfaction with a job well done visible on her face. Chiamanda rubs her hand over her scalp wincing at the million and one cuts on her head. They could have done this at day break.

The tradition that dictates every aspect of life in the Niger Delta demands that a woman's hair be shorn when her husband dies. Chiamanda wonders if this is to make the widow less attractive, to shame her or to take something else away from her. As if losing your husband in his prime is not the ultimate dethronement of a married woman.

'Are you really going to shave my armpits and the hair down below?' she asks. 'How does that appease the gods?

What do the gods do with my hair? Do they burn it as some dumb offering?' From the looks on their faces, Chiamanda knows she has said a little too much.

It was difficult not to question the ways of her people when she was learning new ways of being from the pale skinned visitors. They had arrived long before her grandparents were born and before their parents. They showed no sign of leaving, when one group got old and tired or fever got the better of them, another group arrived.

'Remember our ways are what sets us apart from the visitors,' her mother said when she decided to stop wearing her *Adala*. She'd been wearing the brass anklets since she had come of age. Growing up meant wearing the ridiculous circles of brass around each ankle. Walking was a nightmare as each leg had to swing wide and clear of the other to avoid tripping over.

To people of the Niger Delta, tradition is everything: it dictates what you eat, and your position in life. It governs when you come of age, and when you do, the caste you can marry from and what happens when that union ends.

Coming of age meant she could no longer wrestle with the boys in her age group, climb trees for the fun of climbing, and she had to get married. That bit she didn't mind, as her husband, Nduka, was a great catch. He spoke the visitors' language and knew their ways. His hard work on the farm meant she, and the two sons she bore him, never went hungry. She taught him all that her mother had passed onto her. How to source and make potions for the *fluenza*, and how to cure a fever with lemongrass and bark from the Cinchona tree.

As a boy he had been sent to school to make up the numbers. None of the other chiefs would send their children. 'Why learn another man's language and customs when our customs serve us well?' they said. And so Nduka and others like him – born of slave women and free men – learnt to read and write before the free born.

Nduka was chosen to be the 'ears' of the king of Opobo, the centre of palm oil production in the delta. King Jaja liked his humility and his ability to switch from his native Igbo to the harsh sounding vowels of the English and German visitors.

The visitors never come into the village unannounced. On the day they brought the news, their runners came panting into the square like pregnant dogs. Their Khaki shirts dripping with sweat and the fine red sand that announced the arrival of the harmattan season. On that day, the curlews began their calls before sundown causing everyone to pause and look at each other with an unspoken question. What are the gods angry about now? Even the dogs that lazed around for most of the day stood with their ears upright as if they could hear something inaudible to everyone else.

Four months earlier, the visitors had announced that King Jaja had been released from exile in Jamaica. They had been tricked onto the ship that took them to Jamaica. The latest was that the king and his manservant Nduka had died in Tenerife on the last leg of their journey home.

Before she can run, Chiamanda is banished to the store room in her compound. Thirty days of confinement begin without warning. Her mother looks on helplessly as the *Umunna* – older womenfolk surround her like mother hens, telling her what she can and cannot do. Delighting in her terror and their misplaced importance.

At sunrise, a young girl she'd 'bought' from a middleman a few days back brings her food. Two pieces of cocoyam, a pinch of salt, and red palm oil. Crisscross blisters cover the girl's back. Her skin is the colour of the pale kola nuts.

Chiamanda had found them hiding in the bush; a chain

securing the girl to the man, waiting for sunrise to continue their journey to the place where the River Niger meets the big sea.

'Eight British pounds,' said the man when she asked him to let her go. She offered him five pounds and eighty manilas.

'No-one uses manilas,' he said when she handed them over, throwing them in the dirt as if they were worthless. Paper money has replaced manilas.

'Take it or I report you to the visitor-in-charge.'

He'd picked up the c-shaped iron rings and scurried off back into the bush.

The people of the Opobo say they have stopped the trade, but every war seems to bring people they cannot feed. People with facial scars that should tell them where they come from. People with the same skin colour, whose language their hosts cannot understand. The prisoners of war become slaves and are put to work harvesting the palm fruit for the king and the supercargoes. The supercargoes are the most disliked visitors. They strut about the village, boasting about the money they'll make for their employers in far off places. When the harvest is over, or there are more workers than work, they sell the workers to supercargoes from Cameroon in exchange for British pounds. For material they call Indian madras. For imported gin that makes grown men sleep all day; ignore their crops and do stupid things. And for heavy velvet material soft and redundant in the hot and clammy Niger delta.

After two nights in confinement, Ada and one of the slave girls lead Chiamanda to the stream on the outskirts of the village. Custom demands she bathes at night in waters away from the village. Her friends follow a few paces behind wielding cutlasses and singing praise songs for Nduka.

'Will you shut up,' shouts Chiamanda.

'No amount of praise singing and god pleasing will change what has happened.'

They walk back in silence, her friends watching for night creatures and sleep walking supercargoes.

Chiamanda spends the night in the food store with the mice and the stars for company, a broken piece of mirror ready if required. She is awake before the first slither of light breaks the horizon. It's a time when children are in deep sleep and husband and wives, satiated with the activities of the night, lay splayed like pigs roasting on spits. Even the crickets and the owls are silent. Lone hyenas cackle in the distance, searching for food, a mate or anything to keep them busy before sunup. She watches night turn to day. She can make out the shapes of hunters with their quivers of poisoned arrows, antidotes in small gourds around their waist. Their knives are sharp and holstered. The leather amulets around their biceps hide magic potions said to make them invisible. If she can see them, surely others can too. They move like shadows, merging into one another, noiseless footsteps sure on the ground.

As a curious child, she once followed a group deep into the forest. She watched as the bramble yielded to their cutlasses like warm fingers through shea butter. She watched them scale trees and collect honey without being stung. She saw grass snakes dive for cover, and tree monkeys hide their young. They led her round in circles until she came face to face with a wall of bare-chested men.

'Who saw you?' shouted the tallest, his morning breath almost knocking her over.

'It's an abomination for a woman to hunt with men.'

'No-one. I couldn't sleep,' she said.

Nduka, then a 15-year-old strapping lad, pointed out that

she was not yet a woman. They let her go. She managed to evade slavers and hunters by following the same path back. She followed the honeyguide birds that fed on the wax in the bee's nests on the outskirts of the village. She slept underneath piles of leaves between the buttress roots of *Iroko* trees. She counted two sunsets; she was home before the third.

The visitor-in-charge holds court in the village square. He says they died in Tenerife. Someone put poison in their tea. 'Why poison them now?' ask the people. The orderlies stand to attention, sweating like trussed up pigs, batons at the ready, one eye on their people the other on the visitor-in-charge. From her confinement, Chiamanda can hear the questions fired at the visitor-in-charge:

'Where is this Tenerife place?' they ask.

'Was he not a protected British citizen?'

'How come the governor-general let our king die?'

'They did five years in exile, only to die on the way home.'

'Why were they drinking tea? Is Tenerife cold?'

'Where are their bodies? We must bury our king. If there is no body, there is no palm oil.'

'He must have known the end was near,' she says to the ants marching across the hard mud floor of the store. He knew how to use the beautiful deadly flowers. He would have known when the time was right. They say the sun shines in Jamaica and people of their colour work the land, while visitor people parade like peacocks. They say stolen people from Bonny, Opobo, and people from where the River Niger meets the big sea can be found in this place. They speak the language of the visitors. If they survived five years in a place like that, then why?

The dogs have gone back to lifting their heads only to avoid being stepped on and wagging their tails when the flies become bothersome. The cuts on her scalp have scabbed over, and the hairs the blade missed are rough against her palm. Her stomach complains and readies itself as the heady aromas of roasting goat meat waft through the village. The meat will not touch her lips as it is taboo for a widow to eat food cooked for the funeral of her husband. Crying is forbidden as her husband was a titled man. The night hides her tears and listens to her questions. Her husband did not die in a war. He was not captured and sold like many before him. There is no body to wash and prepare for the journey back home. To ancestors that did not protect him or the King. She is spared the indignity of sitting with his body, fanning flies and watching a once mighty man rot into nothingness. A man at home with his people and with visitors that do not leave.

The vats used to boil the palm fruit are quiet, the slaves slip away at night. The supercargoes get tetchy. Their employers expect their palm oil consignment and a handsome profit. They pass the time making half-visitor babies, fighting fevers and supping over-fermented palm wine.

On the twentieth day of confinement, the wife of the visitor-in charge visits the village with the twin-girl she adopted. Her long skirt swishes the dust as she walks. She weighs the new-born babies and writes things in her book. She wraps strips of white material around the remains of their umbilical cords. These babies will have belly buttons that stay on the inside. The twin girl sticks to the wife of the visitor-in charge like a shadow. To her people, the Efik and Kalabari, twins are bad luck. They leave them in the forest to perish or be rescued by the visitors that do not believe in the evil of an innocent newborn. Her face bears the scars of inquisitive animals that must have wondered if she would be better off as food.

The girl and the wife of the visitor-in-charge check on Chiamanda. A fine film of harmattan dust covers their clothes. Their lips are cracked like everyone else's. The woman talks slowly, the girl translates. The visitor's wife takes Chiamanda hands into hers and prays like the visitors do. To a God they cannot see, a God they say has a son and is everywhere. A God that does not demand offerings. As she prays, she passes Chiamanda a small brass tobacco box. The box is decorated with Palm trees and coconuts made from mother of pearl. It is marked 'Tenerife, 1891'.

In the box are remnants of dried flowers, dried berries and odd shaped seeds. She knows he must have had a good reason to do it and that she cannot tell anyone. She knows that, one day, the visitors will leave. She knows where to find the flowers and seeds to restock the box. She knows that, one day, her children or her children's children will go to Tenerife, find where they buried him and bring him home.

Chiamanda's twenty-eighth day in confinement comes and goes. The *Umunna* and her in-laws are no longer interested in her. Her scalp is covered with soft fuzzy brown hair. Her age group friends visit and gossip. Her children are well, they tell her. Her once smooth mahogany skin, admired by the village menfolk, is dry and grey; falling like fish scales as she moves.

She dreams of festivals and dances gone by. Of running away. Of picking the good bits from the visitors' way of life and weaving them into her own. Of places far away where, according to the wife of the visitor-in-charge, solid water falls from the sky. Of places where people cover themselves with layers of soft, heavy velvet.

Immigrants

Laila Lock

He called me Sister and my heart pixelated.
A week later a vine field message.
'This is the land of your fathers
And my daughters in a row.'

I had been unmoored for a while
Needed to align

With four daughters in a row.
Stood in azure shallows.
Up to their knees in blousa and jeans
Chaining me in to where
The white shells sparkle
In their curly hair
And the corals had always waved
Since he left
That city by the sea.

My Brother loves the rain,
Justice, and the countryside.
I am his own mirror,
once removed
In the agricultural college.

They said, 'Why are you here?'
Odd choice for a girl.
But Dad didn't tell me
About the track that led to
Cooled, tiled courtyards and soft soled
Grandad waiting for him on that lonely

Farm forever.
Only the time he sold the gummer sheep
As gimmers in the market behind
Old Grandad's back.
Who, shame red, hit him with a stick.

Dad needed Paris and dances
And the university on a hill
Behind the farm.
But I, by carrying innocent buckets
and planting the seed
Went home for him.

Granddaughters of the Existential Age

Nina Cullinane

All three, closer to forty than to thirty now, reunited over cocktails in a bar run by young people who look like twenty-first century Twiggys and Brandos. The walls are English-tweed green, and they are seated at the far end where there is an air of privacy, although the bar is actually very small. The waiter, with his top knot and carefully sculpted muscles, casts them in the glow of his shockingly sexy gaze, and each of the three gets her share of his jet eyes; each feels the thrill of what it is to be held suspended inside that glow for a few seconds. The power of it buzzes through them and allows them to return his hold as he flirts with them, takes their order and moves on.

They suck at their cherry cocktails through paper straws. All three with bobbed hair of differing lengths and colours; black, auburn, golden brown. Hannah's curls are slightly chaotic, cut towards her shoulders in a flattering way; Iris and Jo both poker straight with varying degrees of thickness and lustre. At school, they were known as the three sisters, which to them translated as three witches because it always felt like them against the world.

They talk about how the boyfriends could do more, about how they could turn off TVs and laptops and games consoles, fight bad bosses for better hours, help out after work, cook, clean, have the kids more often. And did they mention that they never get to go for nice walks with the boyfriends? Only Iris gets to go for walks at all, which are always ruined by arguments with her academic boyfriend who challenges her on every point, and yet she loves the challenge and knows that's part of the attraction.

They talk about how they don't seem to have found *those* kinds of men, though they've supposedly been popping up all over the place since before they were born. They suck keenly at the straws.

'What do I have to do to get one?' Iris asks, grey eyes glinting, her sable hair gleaming under the chandeliers.

'Fay's got one,' Hannah says, smoothing a stray curl, 'stay at home dad, does everything while she's at work and then studies for his degree at night.'

'God. It must be this town,' laments Jo.

'*Armpit... or Arsehole?*' Iris' grey eyes twinkle. Her strong make-up and hair give her a Cleopatra look, as the other two have always told her.

They each suspect, privately, that they are either too demanding, or not enough. They don't understand the men; the ones they've picked. They feel like they don't really know them at all, only some of the time. And, perhaps, that is the attraction. This allows for the things at which they excel: speculation, angst, despair. They are so far into the woods that it's impossible to see the trees; this they have said to each other. Online reading tells them to raise their expectations, they're being let down because they *allow* themselves to be let down. 'The problem is with me,' each one has said to herself; choosing the wrong one, trying to mould him into a shape that doesn't fit.

'And now the whole world is getting married,' Iris whines, her eyes twinkling furiously. 'Why is marriage still even *a thing?*'

'I like marriage,' says Hannah, 'I want to get married.'

'Puke,' Iris says, motioning with two fingers.

Hannah has told Jake that they're getting married. She wants it all: the public declaration of love, the making of a pledge. She wants to be clear with him so that he knows, when the time is right, that he can pop the question. She wants everyone to share in their love and for people to go away completely bathed in that love.

Iris, on the other hand, couldn't give a toss; third generation feminist; separated parents living streets apart, and Jo isn't bothered either way. Surely, a relationship must be fully tethered to enter into anything that long term? She's not sure hers is tethered since the baby rocked the boat and still hasn't found its keel yet.

'Maybe it's a biological thing: boys are selfish, girls are givers,' Hannah says.

'My mum is the most selfish woman I've ever met,' Jo cuts in, her small red lips perfectly complimenting her neat golden hair. 'She used to make me scrub the front step. Who does that, apart from the Victorians?'

'I can't imagine either of you married!' Iris' voice turns down a notch, 'to *Ben* and *Jake*, I mean you've been together forever anyway...'

Jo leans in and says in a low, conspiratorial voice, 'Ben slept all day last Sunday after his night out with the boys. We were meant to go to Amazon World but he was too *hungover*.'

The other two shake their heads and roll their eyes. Hannah takes her turn to lean in.

'On my thirty-fifth,' she says, 'remember I took the day off work to go for lunch with Jake? He was so hungover from his work do the night before that he spent all morning being sick. So I made him stay at home and went with mum instead.'

Iris and Jo have leaned in too, forming a scrum of disdain, taking big slurps on their cocktails.

Iris calls the waiter over. She deliberates over his recommendations. A round of blackcurrant and mint-sprigged drinks arrives.

'It's the mums,' Iris hisses, 'picking up after them, letting them get away with it...!' her grey eyes bulge with contempt. 'I went out with this bloke years ago,' she says, brushing a hand over her hair, 'whose mum asked me to do the washing up when I stayed over. But it was his turn, not mine!'

The others wait to see if her story will have another act, take a turn for the worse.

'What, that's *it*?' Jo frowns.

'Yeah,' Iris laughs, 'It's a metaphor isn't it... Mother passes chores on to the girlfriend.'

'Yeah exactly, society has a lot to answer for!' Jo, who studied sociology on a night course, shouts. 'It's not the fault of those men or those mums. It's *society's* fault.'

'Yeah,' says Iris, who ran away to university to get a degree, and came back with *a shed load of debt and even stronger opinions* according to her mum. 'But if the mothers didn't keep it going, and all of *us*, letting them get away with it, it wouldn't be so *bad*.'

'What can we do?' Jo shrugs.

'Go on fucking strike!' Iris says.

'I would love to,' Hannah grimaces, 'but the house would fall apart after one day.'

'They should do an experiment, like *I'm a Celeb*, make a fly on the wall TV show...' Jo says.

'Aggghhhh, can we talk about something else?' Hannah, who has been up since four with her three year old, glares at them and smiles as she sees the three sisters re-surface, the ones who had time to argue and complain, and give a shit about stuff. She is already half way through the second cocktail and feels swimmingly good considering the early rise and the sore throat that lingers like spiky weeds around her throat. Something is bubbling up inside of her. Something that's been irking her all of the time but that she holds and holds to keep the peace.

And did they mention the issue of having more babies, or none at all? Running out of time to make this decision has come as a shock to all three; time seems to speed up, although you still *feel* young; still *look* young, relatively speaking. Iris isn't sure she wants to be that consumed by a thing. Totally lost to motherhood. She has seen it consume her friends; willing participants yet lost inside it, it's a rare thing to be meeting up like this.

'I'd love another one,' Hannah's eyes glimmer, the copper-red tones in her hair gleaming under the lights.

The other two think about how good she looks considering the early mornings, but they can see the sadness there too, the sadness of two-years trying to conceive.

'One's enough,' Jo says, 'I cannot imagine having two with work and *everything* else.'

'I would have made a great father,' Iris says with a resolute grin, taking a long slow slug of her cocktail. 'Your kids can come to me with their problems and *angst* and I will be their strategist in this rudderless world.'

Hannah worries about test results. She tells them that the doctor didn't get in touch when he said she would and now she has to wait all weekend for the outcome of her day-three bloods, which project an overall picture of fertility health. But above all, she's concerned that the switch-on-switch-off humping that's become the norm will soon become par for the course; that her entire sex life will revolve around these small windows of opportunity, and the anxiety of whether or not another baby will ever actually happen. She always wanted two, but life got in the way; things had gone off course and now she is determined to make up for lost time. Just one more, if you're listening please God.

In fact, now that she's here with the girls again, she feels the overwhelming urge to share something that's been eating at her. She leans in towards them as she speaks:

'Jake couldn't get it up for a whole month. He just went off sex *completely*, but when I asked him he wouldn't say a thing. *Nothing*.' Her cheeks flood crimson.

'Ohhhh... That's all the trying to conceive honey,' Jo soothes, 'It takes its toll on *them* too.'

'But we're never going to get anywhere if he can't even get it up,' Hannah's cheeks are blazing, her eyes aflame. 'The one thing I ask of him, *and he can't even fucking do that*.'

The other two sit in silence, taken aback, Hannah usually being the placid, level headed one of the three.

The heat of despair pulsates through Hannah. She takes a slug of her drink and exhales deeply. She thinks about how she will drive up the Downs tomorrow and let out the howl that is ravaging through her, threatening the peace of her whole neighbourhood. She remembers the previous scream when it had all gotten too much – the sheer dependency on one person for *everything*; for love, for another baby, for your *entire* mental wellbeing – so she'd just opened her mouth and let it out. Lily started wailing, and Jake said it was like living with a raving fucking lunatic.

'Sorry,' she whispers, 'I'm a bitch. Just call me *bitch*.'

They shake their heads in unison, auburn-gold swaying together.

'No you're not,' Iris leans in, placing a hand on Hannah's, and saying, very seriously, 'You just need a bloody good screw.' They roar with laughter, and order a round of some obscurely named thing. The sexy waiter brings the drinks, creamy white and dense looking.

'Are we having an existential crisis?' Iris shouts over the crowd that has built up in the bar.

'Definitely... ' Jo shouts back, 'Wait, what's existentialism again?'

'Post-god world where everything is meaningless and random,' Iris says.

'Fuck yeah, that's us!' Jo screams.

Hannah slumps in her chair, her hazel eyes swimming.

'Alcohol is our only hope,' she slurs a skewwhiff smile, feeling like the weight that sits on top of her has momentarily lifted, imagining herself scampering up the Downs later that night like a werewolf to howl at the sky. No one will know it's her own howl piercing the silence as she inhabits that wolf with every fibre of her being, running wild over the chalky path down into the fields and the woods; the stiff little bodies of the goats that graze there frightened half to death. The inhabitants sleeping in nearby houses will rouse and wonder what kind of animal could make such a sound.

Love Apples

Liz Houchin

Three days after Christmas, in a semi-detached house in Dublin, Barbara laid to rest the carcass of her twenty-third turkey. This was how she measured the passing of time, a much more respectable number than her age. Both her children had brought friends home from college who had nowhere else to be, and she was grateful for their animation and their appetites. They were now gone to drink in the New Year in some unsuspecting country house. Her husband had nipped to the office to check on things, so she finally had the place to herself. She worked from home as a literary agent and spent the morning responding to emails from her authors – a mix of good wishes and existential despair – and over lunch she ordered tomato seeds: *Gardener's Delight, Sungold* and a new black tomato, *Indigo Rose*, because you only live once.

Her love of tomatoes began on a hot July afternoon fifty years previously when her mother, on seeing the shadow of the health visitor at the door, shoved a carton of tomatoes in front of her as she sat on the grass in nothing but a pair of frilly pants. The health visitor had come to see Barbara's baby brother, who had spent his first weeks in an incubator. As she was packing away the tools of her trade, she looked over from the kitchen chair that was moonlighting as garden furniture.

'Well, you'll never need to worry about her appetite,' she said.

Her mother followed her gaze to the orange rivulet running down Barbara's chubby torso and the empty carton resting on her head of blonde curls. For the rest of the summer, anytime she was asked what she would like to eat, Barbara would simply say 'meat and mat,' translated as ham and tomatoes. Barbara had eaten them almost every day of her life.

Six weeks later, on Valentine's Day, Barbara stood in her ancient greenhouse and turned on the AM/FM radio that still had its original batteries and never minded a dusting of compost or a splash from a watering can. The midmorning presenter was reading out the winning entry to a love poem competition, the subject seemingly a labradoodle named Billy. It was quite touching really.

Barbara got to work sowing her tomato seeds in the same little pots as last year. It was her favourite gardening job; the promise of new life and better weather. She knew they would germinate, as sure as she knew the authors who would turn in their manuscript before the deadline and the ones who would put all their creative energy into excuses and lies, some of which were exceptionally good and could easily have been turned into flash fiction or perhaps a haiku. February was holding on to winter with both hands, and a fierce westerly rattled the fragile aluminium frame that threatened to simply crash to the ground one of these days. Two of the windows were held together with packing tape. Just as she was watering the pots, her husband appeared and coaxed the door open wide enough to pass through a shocking pink orchid.

'Happy Valentine's Day!' he said, flushed.

'Well thank you, this is a surprise,' she put down her watering can and leaned over for a kiss, careful to keep her hands away from his suit.

'I was in the shops and thought you'd like it.'

'You went to a shop? Well there's a first time for everything. I'll just finish up here and get us some lunch.

You can tell me all about your adventures in retail.'

'Actually, I've to run back to the office, but I'll be home for dinner.'

She tore the heart printed cellophane from around the plant and watched him sprint away. While the colour of the flower was mildly offensive, she was grateful for his sudden rush of blood to the head. She felt bad that she hadn't bought him anything, but he valued a good meal above most things. She looked forward to a steak dinner and a glass of wine, but by the time he came home his mood had changed and when she thanked him again for the orchid, he seemed embarrassed, almost like it had been a lapse of judgement that he hoped everyone would have the decency to forget.

A month later, she decamped to the greenhouse on a Saturday morning to transplant the seedlings into bigger pots. Holding one of the first true leaves between her fingers she used an old pencil to lift the white thready roots from the soil and move them to their second home where they would have room to spread out and support five feet of vines. She repeated this action over and over while reading a draft of her favourite author's new novel, covering it in brown thumbprints. It was getting harder to sell books written by people who remembered life before the Internet but this one would be difficult to ignore. She hoped it would remind people that, like the mock orange she had planted beside the front door, some of the most beautiful flowers bloomed only on old wood.

Pausing to turn the page, she noticed her husband on his phone in the shed at the end of the garden. There was no reason for him to be in there and he seemed quite agitated, pacing about as much as anyone could pace in a shed. Their shed was a damp gloomy place where DIY dreams went to die, so Barbara kept her gardening tools in the greenhouse.

He must have been aware that she could see him, so that evening she asked him if everything was alright.

'I saw you on your phone in the shed.'

'Yes, yes, just work, trying to persuade HR to bend the rules for a new hire.'

'Right. I thought it was something more dramatic.'

'Colonel Mustard in the shed with a screwdriver. Not everything's a murder mystery you know.'

'I was thinking more along the lines of a suburban thriller – disguised as a middle-aged accountant, a secret agent takes down the head of the residents' association who is, of course, a war criminal.'

'Nothing that exciting I'm afraid. Anyway, I'm going to pick up some notes from the office that I should review before Monday. Need anything?'

On the second Sunday in April, it was warm enough to have lunch in the garden. Barbara brushed down two garden seats for the first time that year and stole a cushion from the kitchen to insulate her behind from the damp. Nothing signaled summer's approach like eating outside. Pointing out new tulips she had planted the previous autumn, or planning a holiday, they would sit and chat and laugh. But not this time. Her husband was just back from a two-day business trip, and all she felt was a tightness in her chest that had been quietly building for weeks. She had considered a rare visit to the GP, but a phone call the previous day had diagnosed the problem and it was time to share. She put down her fork.

'So, when are you going to tell me?'

'Sorry?'

'Yes, you should be, but I doubt you are.'

'What?' he kept his focus on his plate.

'The estate agent called with some good news while you

were away. He has someone on his books who is interested in viewing our house. I thanked him warmly. He must have assumed that the house was in both our names and that I knew it was going on the market.' She picked up her fork and returned to her quiche. Her heart was now bouncing off her ribcage.

'Oh Barbara, I was just making enquiries,' he said, 'I was going to talk to you first, but I was waiting for the right time.' He reached out his hand and placed it over hers.

'It's all just happening so quickly,' he softened his voice, 'I didn't plan it. God knows I would never want to do anything to hurt you. It's just one of those things. We met at work and she –'

Barbara pulled her hand away, put her finger to her lips and shook her head. She read books for a living. She had skipped the first few chapters, but she knew how this story ended. She took her cup to the greenhouse and gave all her attention to her tomato plants, pinching outside shoots and tying in stems, wiping away washes of tears with her sleeves. She stayed there until she heard his car leaving.

Three weeks later, she was driving back from the solicitors, her marriage all but over. She had stayed standing during the meeting, refused tea and used her own pen. She wouldn't know how she felt for a long time. Turning on the radio to drown out the morning, she caught the end of her favourite song from her college days. She wished she could hear it from the start. Barbara had a habit of playing a song again and again until it keeled over. It drove her husband crazy. He would plead with her to play something new. 'But everything I need right now is in this song,' she would explain. It was how she felt in her greenhouse, with potting compost under her fingernails and in her hair, searching for a packet of seeds that she just had in her hand, or finding shoots that had pushed their shoulders up through the dark overnight and were now lifting their heads to the light.

She parked her car but didn't bother going into the house. Straight through the side gate, stripping off her black, don't-mess-with-me jacket and flinging it on a bench. She pulled her earrings from her ears, kicked off her shoes and slid her feet into a pair of ugly rubber garden shoes that she would like to be buried in. Her tomato plants were now three feet high and covered in tiny yellow stars, but the leaves were drooping and the soil was dry. She started plant triage immediately and swore that nothing else would get in the way of their care.

The house sold without having a sign erected beside the front gate. She was thankful for that, but it meant that she only had a month to leave. Her husband was already holed up with the woman who made him feel young again so he just wanted the cheque. He had also promised the children the panacea of a generous cash gift so lots of helpful pressure was applied to get Barbara out of the house, including a bargain bin mindfulness book entitled '*Moving on with Joy*'. She mindfully shredded each page and sprinkled them on top of her grass clippings.

She found an apartment that she could just about afford. As she signed on the dotted line, she said a prayer that one of her authors would have a bestseller at some point before she died. She did not canvass anyone's views on the property, and couldn't explain why she chose it. Nor would she share her new address widely until she was settled, fearing that a single *New Home!* greeting card would be enough to send her into a deep decline.

Barbara would not accept a suggested late May or early June deadline to leave the family home. Did these people know anything about how tomatoes actually grow? In the middle of June, she fielded phone calls from both her children. Clearly, they had held summit talks. Did they think she was holding out for a reconciliation? She walked out to the garden and balanced her phone on the edge of the compost heap so she could deadhead *Rosa 'Graham Thomas'* while her son and then her daughter expressed empathy tinged with impatience. Barbara counted the wilted roses with each snip and made the occasional 'I'm listening' noise, eventually pressing the mute button and telling them exactly what to do with their concern.

Finally, it was Sunday, July 2nd. Friday had been her absolute deadline to leave the house, but summer heat had returned, and she needed another 48 hours. Her husband was in Greece so she had simply called the estate agent and said that she needed more time and if they wanted the house they would have to wait until after lunch on Sunday, and no, she wouldn't be answering her phone again.

She woke on the nose of 8.00 am. The day broke quiet– so quiet – and warm. Wandering into the almost empty kitchen, she looked out and saw that the air vents had already opened in the roof of the greenhouse. That was a good sign, but she wouldn't go out yet. She made the last cup of tea she would ever drink in her house. Even with bare walls and most of the furniture gone, it felt like her home. The morning light cast the shape of a sail across the wood floor. By lunchtime it would move to where the table used to be, but by then it would be someone else's light. She drained her cup and got dressed.

She walked out to the greenhouse bringing a big colander and a pair of scissors. Pulling away the brick that held the door closed, she stepped inside, the air filled with the scent of warm, fuzzy tomato leaves – a musty, herby smell with touches of tobacco and lemons. Describing the smell of tomato plants reminded her of a wine tasting event she went to with her husband and how they had giggled every time someone swirled their glass and suggested '*Fresh tennis balls*'. Like bold kids swinging on their chairs and daring the teacher to kick them out. She leaned back against the potting bench and closed her eyes, committing to memory the feeling of glass-hot sun on her face.

Before the year was out, she would hear reports of her ex-husband's first 10K run. His new partner was a list of everything Barbara wasn't. It hurt like hell, but right now she was busy saving her summer. Her first tomato harvest would be her last. The *Indigo Rose* tomatoes were an extraordinary colour. Not quite black, but the darkest shiny purple you could imagine. Most of them had only started to colour but there was a group of three near the top that were as perfect as snooker balls. The *Sungold* cherry tomatoes hung in long bunches like extravagant Mardi Gras earrings, deep orange baubles at the top and fading to bright yellow and then lime green at the bottom. But the *Gardener's Delight* stole her heart, as they always did. Branches weighed down with deep red picture book tomatoes, every one as perfect as the last. She had an hour before the new owners arrived, so she worked her scissors until the colander was heaving. Then she dragged the pots outside, dumped the plants on the compost heap and walked away.

She placed the colander of tomatoes on the passenger seat, the ripest ones resting on top. Her laundry bag was in the footwell, and her hairbrush was in the cupholder. The boot and backseat were packed with all the stuff the movers didn't move. She left all of her big gardening tools behind, but still planned to arrive at friends' houses armed and dangerous with a secateurs and a pair of gardening gloves ready to put manners on an overgrown shrub. She patted the rim of the colander and drove like she was taking her first baby home from the hospital.

The apartment that was now her home had no balcony, but the sun shone through the kitchenette window for a couple of hours each day, at least in summer. Barbara laid the green tomatoes along the windowsill to ripen in the company of a basil plant. She opened the first box labelled 'kitchen' and found a gold-rimmed soup bowl from her wedding china. Her first instinct was to fling it across the room with the force of an Olympic shot-put champion. But instead, she filled it with orange, purple and red tomatoes, still warm from the car and ready to burst.

Kicking off her sandals, she hiked herself up on the hot worktop, letting her feet rest in the sink. Barbara liked to know where she stood (or sat) in the world. Out the window, she could see in the distance the red and white striped chimneys of Dublin Port. That meant the Wicklow mountains were straight ahead of her and her greenhouse was behind. She unfolded a threadbare tea towel, laid it across her knees and let the juices fall.

Sirocco

Donka Kostadinova

Today
I'm wearing the hot
easterly wind –
ribbons of dust
and sand
loop and coil
around my face
until my mouth
becomes the eye
of a storm
you want to kiss

my words halt, stunned
they hide between my teeth –
they go back a long way,
I don't want to lose them

exotic, you want to taste them
smell
try them on
see if they suit your mind
before you commit

your tongue finds a stray –
four syllables to your three,
pin it down on display, spread it –
pretty eyeshadow-winged creature.

you bite it, breast milk dribbles –
from the corner of your mouth
Spit or swallow?
perhaps
it will look better
on the pavement
to be trampled –
undocumented,
it does not belong,
a blow-in

sometimes,
even I forget,
no one understands it,
not even my children.
My mother does.

When I dream, blue poppies soar on my breath.

Family Doings

Clara Maccarini

Sorry, at the gym can't talk, everything ok?
Was Lucy's daughter's reply to her phone call half an hour
ago. Lucy noted how her daughter always seemed to be
busy whenever she wanted to talk. They had not spoken
aside from sporadic texts for over a month now. Was it
always going to be this way?

Lucy thought back to when she was her daughter's age.
She had left home, without much more than a goodbye, to
follow a man she thought she loved and settle in a new city.
That was different, though. She had real, tangible reasons
for wanting to leave her home. Her parents had been
dysfunctional long before she was born, and they had never
done one tenth of what Lucy had done for her daughters.
Yet, there she was, sixty-two years old, sat on the couch of
a flat she could not have afforded had it not been for the
death of her parents; resenting them while longing for their
presence, their approval, their love.

The realisation had come late in her life: that all
everyone is ever truly looking for is their parents'
acceptance. Yet to achieve that, one must first accept the
parents in the first place. Which is why we engage in the
senseless dance of life, trying on different partners and
friends, hoping to find acceptance anywhere but within our
parents, looking anywhere but there. How simple would it
be if such realisation did not occur at so late a stage in one's
life?

Lucy's thoughts rested on her daughter once more.
Would she also eventually have this realisation? Would
she, Lucy, be alive then, ready to offer all her love and

acceptance? Her daughter, Annabelle, had left to study at university four years ago. Truly, she had left long before then, always eager to distance herself as much as possible from her origins. Lucy's husband had also left her, much earlier than her daughter. So, Lucy found herself staring at her phone, sat on her couch every evening after work, longing for some human connection, which she no longer felt she could ask for. Yet, she did not blame Annabelle for leaving. She knew her daughter was at that stage in one's life, where it is allowed, even encouraged, for one to be selfish; to forget about duties and responsibilities so to truly enjoy what life has to offer, if only for a brief spell, before turning into everything one was trying to ignore.

Annabelle would occasionally visit her, during winter and summer breaks from university. Lucy felt a pang of anxiety at the thought of her daughter coming back home. She was looking forward to it, as she missed Annabelle with every muscle of her body. Regardless, the anxiety was still present. She hated it, but she feared her daughter who had achieved so much more than her in such little time. She felt as if Annabelle belonged to a different reality, elevated much above her.

She had always known that her daughter was destined for greatness, ever since she was a little child. Her teachers would say she had amazing talents; one of the brightest students they had ever taught. And truly, Annabelle had never given Lucy any issues in terms of schooling. She had always been a diligent, responsible child and teenager. Never fallen in with the wrong crowd. Never stayed up too late or drank too much – that she knew of. And yet, Annabelle was far from perfect. Her obsession with control scared Lucy, who would have gladly accepted her daughter to be a little less perfect if that had allowed for her to be a little more humane. Instead, with every year that passed,

77

Lucy felt it harder to connect with Annabelle. She was now so far an image from that little child, who was so caring and full of love and affection. She was now the shell of a body, inside of which Lucy could only see critique and contempt towards her, her mother.

Lucy could not wrap her head around how bad the relationship with her daughter had become. How had this happened? And when? Was it when Annabelle's father had left? Was it when she, Lucy, had started growing older? She knew she hadn't been a bad mother. So why was it so hard with Annabelle? The difficult teenage years that everyone talks about were over now, Annabelle should have come back to her mother sweeter than ever; why had that not happened? Lucy had given her daughter everything she needed and wanted, she had been such a better parent than her parents had been to her, so why was Annabelle behaving towards her just the same way that she had behaved towards her own parents?

Six years before, when Annabelle's father left their family, Lucy asked her daughter if she wanted to try therapy to help her navigate what she was going through. To her surprise, Annabelle agreed to it. They found a therapist in their city, an old lady recommended to Lucy by a friend. The therapist asked to meet Lucy before starting to work with Annabelle to understand family dynamics. Lucy agreed to what turned out to be some of the worst sixty minutes of her life.

The therapist asked her questions about her childhood, unravelling memories that Lucy had been trying to forget for forty years. It was as if Lucy had taken all the uncomfortable bits and arranged them into a pile, which she had then relegated to a dark corner of her conscious self, determined never to see it again. She could not gauge

how tall and large the pile was, and that was fine with her.
The therapist's questions required answers, and to provide
such answers Lucy was forced to go back to the pile, and
to go through every layer of it. The pile was shaky and
unstable; Lucy's investigation inevitably caused it to fall
apart. She left the therapist's studio in tears and with a
deep feeling of discomfort, determined never to go back.

Lucy was born in the '50s in a rural area north of the
country. She was the youngest in the family with two older
brothers. Her parents had met during the bombings in the
Second World War. Her mother was working as a nurse,
her father was a doctor, and they had met in a camp for
injured civilians outside the city. After the wedding, her
mother quit her job to stay at home and look after the
house and the children. They had asked Lucy's uncle, a
famous architect, to build their house, which turned out to
be truly eccentric. Shaped as an octagon with a transparent
ceiling on the rooftop and an immense garden filled with
roses, the house was set in the countryside, which, back
in the '50s, was so deserted to make you long for human
connection.
  During the winter, a fog would wrap the entire village
bringing an ominous quality to the lives of its inhabitants.
The house was not the only eccentricity in Lucy's family.
Her father was what most would describe as a guy with
his "head in the clouds". His intellect was superior to
most, and his greatest strength was being able to predict
the zeitgeist to the utmost precision. He became insanely
rich by investing his money in all the right places with
no knowledge of finance, and at a time when investing
money with no guidance was rather uncommon. He started
learning Chinese and Arabic in the forties, anticipating
that these languages would become relevant in the future.

He was, however, not fitted for this world. He indulged in earthly pleasures and developed a significant addiction to chocolate and cigarettes. Lucy remembered walking into his bedroom as a child to find herself immersed in a fog of smoke that resembled the one she could see outside her window, only this fog was accompanied by yellow-stained fingers, holes in the bed sheets, and dad developing throat cancer in his sixties.

She never understood her father. He was always escaping from her. When she was a child, he would pretend to have a twin brother. Every time his twin brother was there, she remembered, her father seemed to be elsewhere. He would often forget to pick her up from school. He would wear socks of different colours. The eccentricity, however, did not bother Lucy. That was her father; it was what made him truly unique.

What she did not like, though, was once, during one of her parents' fierce fights, which she had watched hidden behind the couch, he had grabbed a pair of scissors and threatened his wife, and then started cutting her hair to assert his dominance. What she did not like was how he would forbid her from going outside to play with her friends, or even invite them in the house, as he did not like children. What she did not like was how she had once needed four stitches on her chin after he had hit her.

Lucy's father was controlling. As a child, she wanted to get into the swimming team. Instead, he signed her up for karate. She hated karate, she was the only girl there and hated wearing that stupid white robe. At university, she wanted to study languages. Instead, he signed her up for medical school.

'We are a family of doctors,' he would say, 'if you don't want to become a doctor, you may as well leave this house, but you will not be getting any money from us, rest assured of that.'

Lucy was eighteen and lacking any savings, so she started medical school. She hated it. She was scared of blood and bodily fluids. Her brothers seemed to be doing great at medical school, but for some reason she just could not be like them. She forced herself to study. She passed all her exams and reluctantly decided she would go on to become an anaesthesiologist. But she was tired of living at home. Hers was a tiny village, and she longed for more, for independence. She felt constrained by her family, ignored and oppressed.

One day, she saw a chance for an adventure. She was listening to her favourite radio station, when the radio host announced that he and his co-host were organising an interview evening in a city an hour's drive away from Lucy's village. They would bring on interesting guests, mainly musicians, and give their fans a chance to meet them. Lucy was ecstatic. She waited for one of her father's good moods and begged him to let her go. She would be back home by midnight, she swore. Her father agreed, and so Lucy called her best friend and they started planning their trip.

Naturally, when Lucy met the radio host an October evening in the nearby city, she responded to his confident and routine flirting by immediately falling for him. Unlike him, who came from a bigger city; a man with a job that allowed him to socialise with various people, Lucy had had little to no romantic interactions before then. So, when Henry complimented her hairstyle and coat, she felt like there was nothing else to do but fall in love with the man. He was surprised by her sincerity and lack of cunningness. It felt like a breath of fresh air.

'When can I see you again?' he asked her softly at the end of the night.

'I will come again next week,' she replied, though she

did not know if that was a promise she could keep. But her father was surprisingly unbothered by her request.

'As long as you are back by midnight,' he said.

Henry found Lucy's curfew amusing.

'But you are twenty-one!' he laughed. He was not bothered at the beginning, but it soon became an inconvenience. He was twenty-eight and living on his own. He wanted to go out dancing and stay out late. Instead, he had to spend his Saturday nights driving her back to her village, parking away from her house so her parents would not find out about him, with never enough time to feel like she truly belonged to him.

He introduced her to his mother who loved Lucy's simpleness and earnestness. His friends liked her too, though they could not understand her. Once, Lucy and Henry lost track of time and he drove her back an hour past her curfew. The weekend after, she told him that her father had gotten infuriated at her. She was really scared.

'Why do you stay with them?' Henry had asked, impatient. 'You don't even like Medicine, why don't you just drop out and come and live with me?'

Once the thought had been voiced, there had been no going back from it. She went home that same night and packed some clothes as Henry waited outside her house with the car engine on. He had never seen her house before, and for the first time, staring at that weird octagonal building, he realised how rich she must have been. He was wealthy, but in a subtler way. His family owned a print company; good, reliable money.

Lucy had planned to pack her stuff and leave without saying a word to her family, but at the last minute she couldn't do it. She wanted to explain herself, say goodbye, and say that she would come visit on weekends. She went into the living room where her parents were watching television as they smoked. She immediately regretted her decision. Her father heard what she had to say. Then, with his eyes fixed on the television, he plainly explained that if she were to leave the house and drop her studies to follow some man she had met on the streets, he would no longer consider her his daughter. He would not want her to come visit on weekends; in fact, he did not want to see her at all, and she may as well forget any claim she thought she had on their money. That was worse than him getting angry. She lingered in the doorway, waiting for a reaction or even just a look from her mother. When it was clear that was not going to happen, she lifted her bag and walked out.

Life with Henry was exciting. He was wealthy enough to be able to support them both when retaining his job at the radio station without requiring Lucy to work. She would spend her days reading in coffee shops, strolling through the city's streets, buying ice-cream and clothes. She learned how to cook and would prepare recipes that Henry's mother wrote for her on scraps of paper. She thrived seeing Henry content with their life. He was in no rush to be elsewhere when they were together. Days and weeks and months passed by with nothing shaking their happiness. That was until, on a Thursday in April, Henry's face changed in an instance as Lucy told him she was pregnant.

Adjusting to the changes felt inevitable and, Lucy thought, somewhat easier than she had expected. They both started working at his parents' company, as Henry's job at the radio station would not support a family. Him, up in the board, her, a secretary. There was no real need for her to work, but it just felt natural that, if he had to give up his big dream, her life should also become a little more bitter. She accepted that as she had accepted everything since he had suggested she moved in with him – as a passive spectator of her own life.

Four years passed. Four years since she had last spoken to her parents. Four years since she had been at the octagonal house. She was still in touch with her brothers, who adored Henry. They did not know how things had changed between Lucy and him since her pregnancy. But things had changed, despite how she hated admitting it. Now, whenever Henry was with her, his mind was barely present. He would always be somewhere else, thinking about something else, longing for... Someone else? Was she not enough anymore? She felt unable to give him what his job at the radio had given him for all those years: passion, a sense of purpose, excitement.

She tried buying new clothes that he would like, doing her makeup differently, reading interesting articles in the newspaper and then discussing them with him. She never thought of leaving him, not even once during that agonising year of him pulling away. She never stopped to wonder whether she was truly happy or just ignoring reality since he was the only person left in her life. Ultimately, she had chosen him. *Him over anyone else.* She was the one who had followed him; who had moved to a different city, given up her degree, her friends and family, to be with him. But she was happy, wasn't she? What could she know about love? Maybe that's what love was like after the initial excitement had worn off. And anyway, she now had a child to look forward to.

Especially during the last months of her pregnancy, Lucy would so often get caught up in a vortex of thoughts – she became truly detached from reality. Her thoughts were various, but all with the common denominator of her soon to be family. She would have a child with Henry, a daughter, as she had recently learnt from her doctor. In their new family, Henry would finally find all the passion and excitement he had missed since quitting his job. She would love her daughter, and her daughter would love her. She would finally have the family she had always longed for. How much love was awaiting her! How much joy, and hopes, and dreams that would soon turn into reality. She was eager to start her new life. She was eager to become the parent she herself had never had.

Mother, Woman, Other

Lucy Pearce

Bones blush with beatings of twelve,
She curls at the corners,
Woven from fragile frame and paper skin,
Rotten teeth and hand-me-downs,
    "Did you take this, *girl*?"

Then damp, deadened,
Nerve endings burnt into numbness,
Dressed in silent smiles and lowered eyes,
Privately pained and publicly veiled,
    Daughter.

Five fingers frayed at the tip,
Worn from penury, sorrow, slog,
She is laced corsets and pressed seams,
Turned beds and polished gold,
    Housekeeper.

From waning wax grows adulation,
Hushed words wrapped in needle lace,
Legs, hips, and ravelled hair,
Sourdough and submission,
    Wife.

Inside she moulds without mutton,
Scarcely moaning when wood meets frame,
Nine months and life-long,
Sponge baths and crimson palms,
    Mother.

Shall duties die at her side?
Perhaps in nights of liberated soul,
Of rallied voice and whitened fist,
Of yes and no and yes once more,
    woman.

In darkness brews the loudest truth,
From painted lips with staple holes,
She is power and undiluted mind,
She is courage, she is sagacity and she is
    Woman.

Praying

Ruth Wells

I do not have change for the votive
So I sneak a look;
Alone;
Transgressively I light a flame
It waves to life
It broadcasts my sin in this empty place
As if announcing, in its own luminous voice,
My fault

It takes up space
Disproportionately greedy for the darkness

What does this do?

I pause as wax shifts
Embracing the change from static to fluid
Or maybe just forced to suffer the inevitable

Who is this for?
Placating my need to maintain control?
A mocking reminder that I am powerless
Clueless
Wordless

I long to be able to hold this all more tightly
Pious & obedient

But I am not

It's all
Dusty words
Worn spines
Brittle & broken
Broken & brittle

The Visit

Helen Clark Jones

On sunny days, the neighbours would hold card games in the garden. They'd carry the dining table outside and sit in the shade, drinking tea from the second-best china and playing bridge. I used to climb a tree and watch through the leaves, and that's when I'd see her. Auntie May was a distant cousin of Granny's, but they didn't get on, she wasn't like the other women in the family. I'd hear them discussing her in jealous whispers. She'd escaped the monotony of wifedom and been a 'Career Girl', that's what Granny called her. She owned her own house.

Card table chat was jolly. The men in rolled-up shirt sleeves and the women sweating in faded sundresses, shoes kicked off under the table. Their bunioned feet encased in beige stockings, like worn out sausages. Auntie May sat in the sun, keeping score on the back of an envelope. Cigarette smoke swirling around her cats-eye shades and satin straps hanging down her sleeveless arms. A diamond flashed on her hand as she dealt the cards.

From afar, her glamour was magnetic and I wanted to be close.

She lived in the same street as us, at the other end. It was the furthest distance I'd dare go on my own and it seemed like a world away. I knocked and Miss Wilcott answered, her wrinkled face smiling as she ushered me along a narrow hallway that smelled of flowers and dead cigarettes.

'It's Marjorie's girl!' Miss Wilcott showed me to the back room.

'So it is.' Auntie May sat by the window in a plain grey housecoat. Cold light filtered through the lace curtains, filling the room with an underwater stillness and I knew straight away that I'd made a mistake.

'It's the little girl who climbs up trees and spies on people,' said Auntie May. 'What can I do for you?'

I hung in the doorway, unsure. I thought she'd be pleased to see me. 'I've come to visit,' I answered, because by then it was too late.

'I see. Well, you'd better sit down.' Auntie May nodded to a burgundy-coloured sofa. Without lipstick, her mouth looked papery and mean. 'I hope you're not expecting a biscuit. We don't keep things like that in the house. Some people can't be trusted to keep their fingers out.'

Miss Wilcott squeaked by the fireplace. She had the left-behind look of a china doll in a junk shop, her rumpled clothes blending with the ashes in the empty grate. 'That's not fair!' Her voice raised in protest. 'I don't do that.'

'Yes, you do,' said Auntie May. 'You're a mouse. A greedy little mouse.'

I laughed, but it didn't feel like she was joking. The bumpy pattern of the upholstery pushed into my legs.

Auntie May's house was a mirror image of our own, the rooms were exactly the same but on opposite sides, like a coat put on back to front. Our house felt like it never changed. The carpets were worn and there were grubby stains around the switches, where generations of fingers had flicked on the lights. The only new things were the knocks and scrapes made by the people who lived there. But Auntie May lived in gloomy splendour and even though she only had a few ornaments, they looked like they'd been arranged on purpose and they looked expensive. Better than the cheap souvenirs and chipped vases we had at home.

Two bronze figurines stood on either side of the mantelpiece. Glamorous ladies with painted faces and pencil thin eyebrows. The ladies smiled, bending backwards in impossible positions and standing on their toes like gymnasts, showing off their golden legs and fanning out their pleated skirts. They posed together, but danced apart, frozen in the same exuberant dance. The only movement was the mantel clock that stood between them. The pendulum swinging from side to side, first to one lady then the other, ticking off the minutes with an endless, plodding rhythm. Politeness trapped me on the burgundy sofa and I wondered how long I'd have to stay there, until I could leave.

Miss Wilcott leaned towards me, tilting her head like a curious bird. 'It must be hard to make friends,' she said. 'Now that you live in a street where there are no other children.'

It was true. My face burned and I pushed my hands under my legs, against the prickle of the sofa. School nights I could manage, but the loneliness of weekends and the holidays felt endless. In search of company, I'd become a serial visitor and my targets were old people, neighbours who I'd decided had the time to listen and a ready supply of biscuits. People who wanted nothing from me, but the pleasure of my company. I'd chatter away until the fading light, or their glazed expressions, told me it was time to go home. I wasn't used to scrutiny.

'Nobody here but us old ladies.' Auntie May laughed without humour and the diamond on her finger sparkled in the bitter light. 'Got to take what you can get, I suppose. Like we all do.'

'Where do you go to school?' asked Miss Wilcott. 'Is it where you used to live? It's a long way off, I imagine.'

Auntie May listened with interest, waiting for my answer.

'Moreton Street.' I shuffled on the rough upholstery. I didn't like the prying questions. Don't wash your dirty laundry where people can see, that's what Granny said. We don't want people knowing our business. But it seemed Auntie May and Miss Wilcott already knew about us. They knew why we'd gone to live with Granny in the middle of the night. They knew we'd left everything behind and now they were digging for more. But Auntie May was family. I didn't know about Miss Wilcott.

'Moreton Street?' Miss Wilcott looked up as though the answer was written on the papered ceiling. 'Isn't that on the other side of town? How do you get there? Do you take the 47 bus?'

'The 47?' Auntie May hooted. 'What are you talking about? She'll take the 36 then change to the one-two-nine, by the precinct. Why on earth would she take the 47?'

'But the 47 stops on Gibson Street. It's only a short walk.'

'We go in the car,' I said. 'Mum works next to the school. She says it's best if we're in the same place. She can keep an eye out then. Just in case.' My face burned. The conversation was veering close to dirty laundry and I didn't know how to stop it. I fidgeted on the scratchy sofa. The figurines posed on the mantel, their sharp white teeth shining under ruby-painted smiles.

'I like the ladies,' I babbled. 'I like their dresses.'

'The 47 goes nowhere near Moreton Street!' said Auntie May. 'What a ridiculous notion. Go and fetch the timetable, it's in the drawer.'

Miss Wilcott hesitated, reluctant to give ground. Then she got up, smoothing her ash-coloured skirts, and left the room. She had a slight limp I hadn't noticed before and I wanted to run after her, escape down the darkened hallway and into the street. But I didn't.

'Did you see that?' Auntie May glowered at Miss Wilcott's empty chair. Opposite, but smaller, and lower than her own. The arms were shiny from years of use. The seat had a sunken hollow and a hand-knitted cushion crumpled under the backrest.

'Did you see how she got up?' said Auntie May. 'She does it for attention. Likes to make out she's in pain. She's got a problem downstairs.' She jabbed her fingers to the carpet, leering. 'With her waterworks.'

I didn't want to think about Miss Wilcott's waterworks. I wanted to go home.

'I took her in.' Auntie May pressed her lips together, squeezing them tight, trying to reel me in on the tide of her loathing. 'I put a roof over her head. I gave her a home and what thanks do I get? She wants you to feel sorry for her.' She half-closed her eyes like she was relishing something delicious. 'Don't give her the satisfaction.'

The pendulum swung between the dancing ladies, filling the silence, and I traced the arm of the sofa, noting the pattern of flowers. Counting the petals while furtively taking in the patches on Auntie May's housecoat. The clumsy darns on her stockings. Willing Miss Wilcott to come back.

She returned, clutching the timetable, and her eyes flitted between me and Auntie May, checking to see what had changed.

'You've brought the wrong one.' Aunty May snatched the folded pamphlet, without even looking, and threw it aside. 'It's last year's, what good will that do?'

'It was in the drawer,' said Miss Wilcott, 'like you said. But there's no point in keeping it, if it's out of date. You should throw it away.'

Auntie May sucked on her teeth. 'Go and fetch the other.'

'If you're so sure where it is,' said Miss Wilcott. 'Go and fetch it yourself.' She sat down, folding her arms.

My heart raced. I rubbed my sweating palms on the burgundy sofa. 'I think I should go now.'

'Stay where you are!' Auntie May and Miss Wilcott spoke together. I clutched my hands in my lap as they faced each other across the unlit fireplace. Auntie May's glasses shining in the cold light and Miss Wilcott's fingers gripping the arms of her chair.

I thought of my visits to the neighbours. Mr and Mrs Jackson's cake tin, the sweets in Mrs Thorley's cupboard, the thrilling back and forth of Miss Benson's rocking chair. I wished I'd never set eyes on Auntie May.

Then Auntie May sighed. 'Alright.' She left the room.

Miss Wilcott's gaze burned into me, like a pin through a butterfly. 'I know she was talking about me when I was out of the room, you know.'

I looked at the closed door, desperate to escape. Unable to move.

'She thinks she's the queen,' said Miss Wilcott. 'She puts on a good show, but she can't afford it. It's me who pays for this place.' She leaned towards me, her little face sharp and triumphant. 'She'd be nothing without me. And she knows it.'

The door swung open and she fell back, snapping her jaw shut and looking up at the ceiling in a pretend act of innocence.

But Auntie May ignored her. She ignored both of us. She flicked through the latest timetable, nodding at the numbers. Then she threw it on the side with the old edition, as though the whole thing hadn't mattered at all. The clock chimed the hour and, although I'd only been there a few minutes, I felt like I'd been there forever.

I stood. 'I really have to go now.'

'But you'll want to see the flowers before you leave?' asked Miss Wilcott.

'Oh, yes!' Auntie May clapped her hands. 'You must see the flowers.'

We walked in a line down the dingy hallway, me at the back. Auntie May entered the front room and threw back the curtains.

'There,' she sighed. 'Aren't they just glorious?'

Sunlight flooded through the bay window and blazed on curling red petals, pointed sprays of lemon yellow and soft pink pom-poms shot through with daggers of emerald leaf and pale green fern. The scent was overwhelming. Vases and vases of flowers in silver bowls, two-handled urns and coloured crystal, arranged on side tables, stools and dining chairs, filling the entire room. Jagged shadows fell on the floor and crawled through the jungle of wooden legs. Dramatic spires of orange and white in sparkling cut glass, bloated stalks turning yellow in cloudy liquid and underneath the sickly smell of flowers, stagnant water mingled with the stink of rotting stems.

Each arrangement had a note tucked among the flowers, handwritten on a little white card: Rest in Peace.

'They're from the funeral home,' breathed Miss Wilcott. 'They don't cost us a penny.'

Auntie May clasped her palms in wonder, gazing at the floral scene. 'And they bring us such joy!'

It was several weeks before the loneliness of the summer holidays gave me the courage to visit again. But I found the curtains drawn and a 'For Sale' board by the front gate. There had been a nephew, apparently. Ernest. He'd turned up even before the funeral had taken place and cleared everything out. Some people had no shame, that's what Granny said. He'd taken the lot.

I peered through the letterbox along the darkened hallway. A shaft of watery sun fell through the window over the door and swirling dust sparkled in the silence. The house was full of nothing but shadow. I thought of the dancing ladies on the mantelpiece, the ghoulish flowers quietly dying in the front room, and the knitted cushion, crushed and defiant in the empty chair.

'But what about Miss Wilcott?' I asked later. 'Where did she go?'

'You mean the lodger?' Granny sniffed and filled another clue on the crossword, taking her time. 'I have no idea.'

Thought-washing
Denise O'Hagan

There are no words for dawn, only
    For its effect on us. The winter light
Swilled, ink-blue morphing linen grey
    To white, soaking the thickened window pane,
The cracked seats of the London-to-Brighton train,
    My chapped hands, my feet; no stained-glass
Window ever streamed
    A light so sweet.

I hung out my rags of thoughts, freely
    In air before me – the maimed, the
Soiled and stained, and watched them sway
    In time with the train: the ghosts we carry,
So fretted and frayed, yet pressing through
    The solid people of this world.
And all the while,
    The white light shone.

And days later, I found
    I couldn't ignore myself any longer.
What we were was slowly disengaging itself
    From the idea of us: had you noticed?
I envied the lovers of literature;
    Romeo and Juliet never got to this point –
But they also were never gifted the chance
    To wash their thoughts clear in the light.

Les Soeurs Jumelles

Fiona J. Mackintosh

(Based on the painting "The Two Sisters" by Théodore Chassériau, 1843)

We were always dressed alike, Maman insisted on it. We were the Thibaudeau twins, never Clothilde and Marie-Bernardine. Our clothes were beautiful, but they were not mine and hers. People said they couldn't tell us apart, but no one seemed to notice how different our faces were – the eyebrows, the hairline, the set of our mouths. Maman and Papa were no exception. To them, we were two halves of the same whole, and let no one dare think otherwise.

Yet the truth of it was, we were not even sisters. When Aunt Hélène was ruined back in '23, by a snuff salesman who passed through Coligny, she flung herself at Papa's feet, begging for mercy. Hearing the pitch of their voices, Maman, already wearing her waistband high, came to decide what was to be done. The world was told of a double *accouchement* in Biarritz, far from home. Maman returned triumphant with two babes in her arms, and months later Aunt Hélène came back from a long stay in the south for her health.

No one told me any of this, but, from the earliest I can remember, I knew I was the seed of Aunt Hélène's sin. I saw her sallow, pointed face in the mirror, no matter how much I pinched my cheeks to make them round and red like Marie-Bernardine's. She was the hearty one, while I was sickly and slow to grow. Maman told me there is always a smaller twin, the one who is pushed aside in the womb by the other, but I knew I'd never been inside that cramped ball of darkness with anyone else.

There could not be a moment's doubt that Marie-Bernardine was everyone's favourite. Maman doted upon her, and Aunt Hélène's eyes followed her wherever she went. Even at school, Marie-Bernardine was fawned on by the nuns, at least by those who could tell us apart. At *récréation*, my twin and her friends prowled around me, the bastard child, the poor relation, their eyes wide like I was a juicy leg of beef or a shiny stone.

After school, I'd run off to play with the *gamins* of the town in exchange for sugar cubes I stole from home. Maman would bring me to Papa for a beating for ruining my clothes. I'd pretend to wail and cry while she listened at the door, but as her footsteps died away, he let me look at his books. I loved turning the thick crackled paper and touching the blue, green, and gold of the illustrations. The beautiful Cassandre in Ronsard's *Odes* and *Amours*, her nose in a rose. Lancelot leaning on the hilt of his sword, dreaming of Guinevere. And my favourite – *the Chanson de Roland*. Papa said it made a nonsense of history, but I cared not one bit. I loved to gaze at the handsome young knight Roland, riding up the mountain pass of Roncesvalles with the gallant Oliver by his side. Often in the swoon before sleep, I seemed to feel the fair Oliver stroking my face while the dark Roland kissed the creases of my palm.

By the time Marie-Bernardine and I were nineteen years old, we were alike in height and had the same black tresses looped fashionably around our ears. Young men came from as far as Rennes and Nantes to ask us to marry, but Maman was always sure we could do better. When people saw us walking with our maid on the *Rue de la Mairie*, they smiled to see the closeness between the Thibaudeau girls, but of our real relations, they knew nothing at all. My twin was everything I was not, and I hated every hair on her head.

When the *Journal* announced that a portrait artist would be coming to Coligny, Maman clapped her hands and said to Papa, 'let's have him paint the girls.' Papa looked over his spectacles and asked her why she thought he needed a portrait of the daughters he saw every day at *petit dejeuner,* but he wrote the letter anyway, offering the painter his hospitality and asking his rates for a three-quarter length portrait with two figures.

The answer must have been satisfactory because we were told the painter would be with us by June. Maman had new dresses made for us from stiff silk in a broad red stripe. They were cut straight across the collar bone in the new style. Concerned that too much of our flesh would show, she ordered shawls of soft red cashmere from Scotland.

There was great excitement in town when the man arrived. Children gathered round the *diligence* to watch the strange-looking easel being handed down from the roof. The painter was dapper and rather full of himself.

At the dinner table, he could not stop looking from Marie-Bernardine to me, and when Maman asked if he was preparing for the portrait, he replied, 'ah no, Madame, it's only that I'm quite a connoisseur of twins. I must have painted a dozen or more in different attitudes. It has quite become my *forté.*' I saw Maman glance quickly at Papa and then down at the glistening oysters on her plate.

The next day, the painter set up his easel in the salon. Aunt Hélène sat in the window seat to chaperone, sewing a hem saver in Maman's riding skirt. The painter winked at us when she wasn't looking. He arranged Marie-Bernardine and me standing side by side against the green wallpaper, slightly turned towards each other, and bade me put my arm through hers. Surveying us with narrowed eyes, he leaned forward and slipped the shawl off my left shoulder.

'Voilà! That's better.'

At first, trying not to move, I stared at the tapestry Papa bought from the estate of a local marquis who'd lost all his money at the tables and shot himself for shame. It showed a *fête champêtre* with ladies and gentlemen lolling in a riot of embroidered flowers. One gentleman played a lute, and a unicorn ate an apple from a lady's palm.

I dreamt myself into that garden of delights, the gentlemen attentive, the ladies coy but willing. Under the rippled shadows of the trees, I seemed to hear birds fluting overhead and feel the cool grapes on my lips. The handsomest of the men turned towards me with a smile and I trembled, but the painter cleared his throat, and I was once again beside my sister, back aching, eyelid twitching with the effort of standing completely still. My damp fingertips marked the crisp silk of Marie-Bernardine's sleeve. Not since childhood had we been so close that our breath mingled, and even then, only when we had scrapped and wrestled over something we both wanted. I knew from the sourness under her arms that she suffered as I did, and I felt sure she could smell my *règles* under my petticoats. I knew she had hers too as I'd seen our rags steeping in the gaudy pink water of the wash tub.

The painter dabbed and daubed. He stepped back to look at us and then at the canvas, a deep frown on his face as if he found us wanting. In an exaggerated tiptoe, Maman entered the room with a line of local ladies in her wake, gratified to show them the great artist from Paris painting her daughters. There was a bustle of maids moving chairs and bursts of whispered laughter as the ladies settled down to watch, pecking at sugared almonds like turkeys in a field.

The painter held his brush out at arm's length and squinted. 'Mademoiselle Clothilde, would you be so kind as to raise your chin just a trifle? *Comme ça – très bien!*'

My neck ached and my feet throbbed in my shoes, and I

felt certain I would faint. As my breathing grew more rapid, I found to my surprise that Marie-Bernardine held me up, her elbow bracing me against her body.

Before I could think what to make of it, the painter said, 'Mesdemoiselles, you may take a rest,' and Maman rang the bell for coffee and cakes. I stepped away from Marie-Bernardine, and her arm fell to her side. Dabbing my upper lip with a handkerchief, I took my coffee to the window seat where Aunt Hélène moved aside her mending to make room.

The painter took a cup from Maman and settled in among the ladies who listened avidly to his chatter. 'I'll never forget the twin boys in Lyon, perhaps 10 years old, a banker's sons. They would not sit still for a moment, not even for sweetmeats. Yet I had exactly the opposite problem with two elderly sisters in Tours who kept nodding off. Time after time, I was obliged to come forward to take them by the shoulders and prop them upright again. I was afraid I might have to draw out a mirror to be sure they were breathing for there was no one in the room but themselves and I, and the maid was too deaf to hear the bell when I rang!'

The Coligny ladies laughed with delight, and Maman looked from face to happy face, puffed with satisfaction.

The painter held out his empty cup to her with a bow, and she filled it from the pot. 'I couldn't tell most twins apart if you threatened me with the guillotine. With some, there's not a hair on their heads or a mark on their skin to show their difference, not in plain view in any event. I do my best to distinguish between them as it pleases the clients. Mercifully, this is not always so difficult to do.'

From my perch on the window seat, I looked down into the courtyard where a drayman's youth leaned against the wall of the house, shirt open at the neck. Glancing up, he whipped off his cap and grinned a gappy smile, and I fluttered my fingers in his direction. Aunt Hélène made a sound, and I braced myself for her reproof, but she was staring intently at the painter who had not stopped talking.

'Take the young Thibaudeau ladies for instance. They are what is known as non-identical twins.' Maman's cup halted halfway to her mouth. 'While the delightful Mademoiselle Clothilde is the very image of her mother, as soon as I entered this lovely home, I noticed that the charming Mademoiselle Marie-Bernardine takes after her noble aunt, Mademoiselle Vannier – something marked about the bone structure. It is to be expected of course. There is a blood relation between aunt and niece almost as close as between mother and daughter.'

As he bowed towards Aunt Hélène in our corner, her mouth dropped open, and suddenly I knew I'd been wrong all my life about which Thibaudeau twin was the bastard. The painter had seen it at once. From across the room, Marie-Bernardine's gaze caught mine, and we stared and stared like neither recognised the other.

In a flurry of nervous laughter, Maman rose to urge the ladies away – 'we have detained our guest long enough. We really must give art its due!' – and the painter stood to bow them farewell. Aunt Hélène looked as if the house had fallen in upon her, her skin grey as distemper.

I leaned close and pressed my hand on hers. 'Don't be afraid, dear Aunt – now all is known, you and she are free to be together.' Her eyes were as large as goose eggs, and I feared a little for her wits.

The painter suppressed a yawn and moved back towards his easel. As he held out a hand to invite us to resume the pose, Maman hurried back into the room, all rustling skirts and hauteur, the colour livid on her cheekbones.

'Monsieur, forgive me, but that must be all for today.

I'm concerned not to overtire my daughters – they are both feeling a little delicate if you understand my meaning.'

The young man paused in squeezing more paint onto his palette and looked from Maman's face to Aunt Hélène's. He put the palette down and wiped his hands on a rag.

'Of course, Madame. I am at your service.' As he turned away to cover up the canvas, he made no attempt to hide his smirk.

By the time I came down the next morning, they were gone – not only the painter and his easel, but also Aunt Hélène and the daughter of her heart. So many empty chairs at the breakfast table. I ate one brioche after another while Maman wept bitter tears for the loss of Marie-Bernardine. Papa's eyebrows were a V above his nose. So rash of them to heed the gossip, he said. It was just the painter's foolish notion. Everyone could see the girls were alike as two peas, and there was the document in his library desk that proved Maman had given birth to twins before her due time when she'd been in Biarritz to take the saltwater baths. And it must be obvious to all, he said, that Aunt Hélène was too sickly to have borne a child, even if any man had been willing to have her. But by running off into the night in fear of shame, they'd made it seem the truth.

Papa shook his head, and Maman wailed, 'We're ruined!' but I smiled into my *tasse de chocolat* and tapped my dancing feet on the floor.

Some years later, we got word that Aunt Hélène had died of quinsy in Paris, and I wondered what had become of Marie-Bernardine. It's possible she was kept by some rich man in a magnificent apartment in the Faubourg Saint-Germain. Or perhaps she lived in an *atelier* with a dirty skylight, scrubbing stains from the underclothes of the bourgeoisie. I knew which one I hoped for.

Now Papa and Maman are gone too, leaving me their only heir. Although I have this fine house and all the money, no one comes to ask for my hand. The townsfolk stopped calling after the scandal, but the servants stay on because I make it worth their while. When I lie abed late in the mornings, resting my book against the stable boy's long, bare back, my eyes are drawn to the frame mounted above the fireplace in which two ghostly, faceless figures are standing side by side. And strange to relate, I feel again my arm through Marie-Bernardine's, the rasp of her silk bodice on the back of my hand, and I find myself missing the sharp, clean smell of my sister's jet-black hair.

Almost Fifteen

Mary Byrne

Rachel could see the man through the living room window. He wore a navy jumper and had short grey hair. He sat in the best armchair by the fire, the seat Grandma always had when she came round.

Her mother opened the front door. She had put on lipstick. 'Come and meet him. He's OK. You don't have to be nervous.'

'I'm not.' That was a lie. 'But I won't know what to say.'

'Just be normal. If you don't want to say anything, don't.'

Rachel hung up her blazer, straightened her school skirt, and followed Mum into the living room.

He wore jeans and trainers. She was disappointed he wasn't more dressed up. He was tall and skinny and didn't look like her, except they both had long noses. He stood and put out a hand to shake hers. She was too embarrassed to touch him.

'I don't suppose you remember me.' His voice was gruff as if he smoked a lot. 'Of course you don't. You were only a baby.'

'She's not a baby anymore,' said Mum. 'Fifteen next week.'

'Quite the young lady then.'

He sat down. Rachel sat on the couch that was so old – second-hand like all their furniture – she sank into it until she was small and he was almost a giant. No one spoke for a few minutes and she had time to have a good look at him. His face was worn, deep lines on either side of his nose, wrinkles round his eyes, but it was kindly. The grey hair was actually white at the front. He'd left when she was two and she had no memory of him.

'Rachel, tell your dad what you're good at in school,' said Mum. 'She's *very* clever.'

Rachel felt herself blush. 'I'm not that good.' He was smiling, encouraging; his eyes were blue – like hers. 'I'm quite good at maths and science.'

'Quite good? She's in the top set for everything.'

'Not everything.'

'What's your favourite?' he said. He sat forward to hear.

'Biology, I think.'

'She wants to go to university,' said Mum.

'Really! That's terrific. What'll you study?' He was staring at her. Well, she'd stared at him.

'Molecular Biology. If I get in.'

His eyes widened and he laughed. 'Wow! I don't even know what that is. I left school when I was sixteen with one 'O' Level.'

She plucked up courage. 'What did you do?'

'Worked in a box factory. I hated it.'

'Yes, but when we met,' said Mum, 'he'd been to evening classes and become an insurance clerk in a nice suit. I was well impressed.' Mum's cheeks were flushed. For a moment, Rachel thought maybe he'd come because they were going to get back together – they must have been talking in order to work out the visit – but then her mother added, 'I was easily impressed.'

'What'll you do with – what did you say – Molecular Biology?'

'She'll work in a lab.' Why did Mum keep speaking for her? 'Discovering genetic things like DNA.'

'Well, I never.'

'Mum, I'm not grown-up yet!'

'You're doing well,' he said. 'I was worried.'

If he was worried, why had she not heard a thing from

him – ever? No Christmas presents, no phone calls, not even a birthday card. He knew they still lived at the same address because Mum got regular Child Support. Her whole life avoiding conversations on what her father did or looked like.

Mum took out a cigarette and lit it. She offered him one but he shook his head. 'Are you still in Ealing?'

'Yes, but I'm moving back.'

'Are you?' Mum frowned.

'Bought a house in Blackpool.'

'Whereabouts?'

'New estate on the way to Poulton.'

'Doing well then. We're still renting.'

'Done it up nice though,' he said, glancing round.

Had they always been like this, talking as though they were people at a bus stop? No wonder it didn't last.

Mum was edgy, taking lots of quick puffs. She seemed to remember something and jumped up, dropping ash on the carpet. 'I didn't make the tea. How stupid can you get. D'you still take sugar?'

He nodded. 'One, please.'

When Mum had shut the door, Rachel wondered what on earth to say. Should she ask him what his job was now? But she didn't have to wonder, for he leant down and pulled a carrier bag printed with flowers from the side of the chair. She could see packages wrapped in pink tissue peeping from the top.

'This is for you. I remembered it is your birthday next week.' He handed the bag across. His hands were like hers, with long fingers. 'You can open it now if you want.'

She took out the first package and began to unwrap it. Her hands trembled. The paper rustled in the silence. Inside was a carefully-folded white blouse. She lifted it out nervously. The neck was covered with frills and embroidery. Not her thing, not her thing at all, though it was very pretty and the right size. It was the kind of blouse a little girl would wear. Did he think she was still a child?

'Thank you. It's beautiful.'

'For a special occasion. A milestone. Like your fifteenth birthday.'

The other package was smaller. Inside was a tin of coloured pencils arranged in neat, bright rows.

'I imagined you'd like art,' he said, apologising when she didn't respond.

'I do! And I can use them for my science and biology diagrams too. Thank you very much. They're great.'

He smiled, looking so sad that for a moment she felt sorry for him. She imagined him in his new house, sitting on a fake leather couch, eating a ready meal in front of a huge TV.

'I wanted to ask you...' He stopped. 'Now that I'm moving back...' He stopped again. 'Would you like to meet up sometime?' So that's what the visit was about. His eyes pleaded. His hands pressed into the wooden chair arms until his knuckles were white. 'I know I've been a terrible father, not really a father at all.'

What was she supposed to reply? Thank you for finally remembering me? But he was her father and she wanted so much to have one, to be a sort of family like everybody else, even if it wasn't perfect.

'I'm different now. I want to make amends. Get to know you.'

She looked down at the pleats of her skirt as if they'd tell her what to do.

'You don't have to decide this minute. Think about it. You could text me.'

'I don't have your phone number.'

He took out a little card, scribbled on the back and

handed it to her. She pushed it into her skirt pocket. Where had Mum got to? She must be leaving them together deliberately.

As if he knew what she was thinking, he said, 'I've talked it over with your mother. I'd collect you. We could go for a walk in the park or go to a film. Anything you want. There's more going on where I am in Blackpool than here if you want to go to my house.'

She pressed her nails into her palms. It was too soon to go to his house.

'And if you come over there, I'd like you to meet somebody.'

He glanced towards the door as if he didn't want Mum to hear. There was no sound from the hall but a cupboard banged shut in the kitchen.

She shivered. Maybe he had a partner or even a wife. She hadn't thought of that. He would want Rachel to play happy families with strangers like some of her school friends did with their parents' new partners. Except they knew their fathers in the first place.

'I'd really like you to meet her. I think you'd get on – you and Amber.'

Amber! She'd be a hippy type like her friend's mother, all floaty dresses and trailing necklaces. *That's* where the frilly blouse had come from.

'What does Amber do?' Rachel said, trying to ask something without committing herself.

'Do?'

'For a job.'

He laughed, throwing his head back. 'No, Rachel, Amber isn't my partner. Amber is my *daughter*!' He paused, then added, 'I mean my *other* daughter.'

It took a few seconds to sink in. *Another* daughter. A real one. One that made a father laugh because she didn't remember. She wanted to cry or even scream.

He was smirking. 'Sorry, I should have prepared you for that. Sorry.'

'Amber...' She swallowed. 'Does she live with you?'

'Yes, of course! And Jessica, her mum, my partner.'

'Does Amber know about me?'

'Yes.'

'But I don't know about her.'

'No, and I wanted to put that right. I want to put everything right. Start again.'

The kettle in the kitchen whistled.

Maybe it would be all right, once she was over the shock. A younger sister. She'd always wanted one. Someone like her – half their genes would be the same. When the little girl was older, they could go shopping or even on holidays together.

'How old is Amber?'

'She's thirteen.' His face was full of warmth and affection. 'Nearly fourteen.'

Nearly fourteen. Something was wrong, really wrong. Only a year younger than her. Her stomach tightened. She did the maths. He had left Mum when Rachel was two; he must have left them because Amber was already there. Jessica instead of Mum, and another baby instead of her. And a nice house, not like this one that Mum had spent years repairing and painting.

'Does Mum know about Amber?'

The warmth in his face died. He bit his lip. 'No.'

'Does she know about Jessica?'

'Not yet.' He wouldn't look at her.

'But Amber's nearly fourteen.'

'It didn't seem worth hurting your mum. She'd already been through enough.'

'Are you going to tell her now?'

'Well...' He pulled at his sleeve. 'It's all water under the bridge. Why spoil things?'

'You don't want me to tell her?'

She thought of Mum stirring his tea with the one sugar. Her mum who seemed to feel there was still some kind of flame between them.

'You're almost fifteen. That's nearly grown-up. I'll leave it to you to decide but don't tell her just yet, mm? It's our secret.'

She had always hated being told 'secrets'. They were like a punishment for the hearer. But this one was more like being inflicted with a terrible disease.

There was the clink of china against metal, and the next minute Mum had opened the door, walking backwards and carrying a tray of mugs and a plate of biscuits, which she handed out.

'Yours is sweet.' Mum smiled at him like a teenager. She caught sight of the blouse. 'That's pretty.'

'For her birthday,' he said.

'Very nice. Very thoughtful. Did Rachel tell you? We're going to have a little party here with a few of her friends. Pizza and ice cream – everyone gets to choose their favourite flavour. Maybe you could come.' She looked towards Rachel for corroboration.

Before Rachel could work out a reply, he said, 'Thank you. That's very kind, but I won't this time.' He gulped his tea down. 'Actually, if you don't mind, I'd better be going. There's a lot that needs doing. Sorting the house and all that.'

They stood. He made to kiss Rachel but she moved back.

'I said I'd like to meet up with Rachel sometime. If she'd like.'

'Good idea.' Mum smiled at him. Her lipstick had smeared.

After he'd gone, Mum ordered a tandoori takeaway. For a treat. As if it was a celebration.

'Are you going to see him?' she asked, smiling meaningfully.

Rachel didn't answer.

'He's nicer than before. It would be such a shame if you didn't. Fathers and daughters, you know.'

In her bedroom, Rachel took out the card. It was shiny and important-looking. On one side, it said, 'Henry Fallon. Independent Financial Consultant' with an email and phone number. On the other, he'd scribbled: 'To my dearest daughter, Rachel. Here's to the future and better times.'

Tomorrow, she'd tell her mother. Sit her down and explain; explain why she wouldn't ever be seeing him again. Her mother would cry and Rachel would hug her as if Mum was the child. She caught sight of the blouse thrown on the bed. She held it against her. It looked like something for a fancy dress party: a fifteen-year-old posing as ten.

She tore the card in pieces, then picked them up from the floor and tore them into even smaller bits.

Mother and Child

Denise O'Hagan

Flesh and blood, 158.5 x 35 cm, 1997, artist unknown

She sat, like we all did, holding him wrapped in
Soft stripes of pastel pink and blue; you could tell
Those hospital blankets anywhere. The air was

Hushed around her, shadowed like the underbelly
Of a mushroom, painting her in the finest strokes of
Pale grey. I held my own complicated bundle of life

Tighter. Things were precarious, more than any of us
Wanted to admit. The nurses trod back and forth,
Watching us, and the clock; our half an hour was

Nearly up. She looked at me then, her eyes dark bruises
Against the shock of her face, and drew her child to
Her breast, swollen with undrunk milk. The blanket

Slipped from miniature limbs, a plastic anklet. Silently,
She pulled the blanket back and shielded him with the
Full curve of her body, brushing his head with her lips.

She would not give up; she would fill the space left
By his unresponsiveness, and tend that which had
Grown between them during their nine short months:

A portrait of mother love, blocked out there in the ward
In its most elemental form, unyielding in the face of fact.
I recognised myself in her, and shivered; she was all of us.

Ménage à Trois
Ekaterina Crawford

There were always three
in this marriage. Me,

you,

and your friend
or so you came to call it.

Hesitant, at first, his visits were rare
and fleeting. Bolder,

with time,

self-assured, he visited more often,
stayed for longer,

became more aggressive.
Aged in Ireland,
matured in Scotland,

He claimed

to know more of the world,
made

you

see things through his eyes, spoke
on your behalf, when you felt tongue-tied,

and made me tremble from your touch.

Meetings, hypnosis, therapy
kept him away for just that long until

one day

I knew –
your friend was here to stay.

We learned to coexist

He and I –
each in our own time.

By day, I still have your love,

but as the sun goes down, your friend
slithers out from his glass lair

as night falls in, I run and hide.

Vermin

Julie Evans

The night before we left for Portsmouth, Mary Anne woke screaming again.

Kezia went to comfort her. If I hadn't known Kezia's character by then, I would never have imagined she could be so kind. I was much afraid of her at first, with her blackened teeth and foul speech. She was clearly Queen Hen in that cell and eyed me with suspicion for several days after I arrived, until she knew that I would be compliant. Hannah told me that Kezia had been the leader of a gang of wild women thieves, well-known for their cruelty to their victims. But she was so gentle with Mary Anne, almost motherly. In truth, we all cared for Mary Anne. She was thirteen; looked ten.

It was pitch black in the cell in the night when Mary Anne's screams rang out. None of us could see her face, but we knew that expression of terror that came over her when she 'saw' Kat Hanrahan.

Kezia cradled her. ''Twas just a dream, Mary Anne.'

Mary Anne whimpered. 'The flames... Her hair was on fire, Kez, all that black hair...'

'Sssh. She's gone now. And we leave tomorrow, little one. Kat will stay here. She won't bother you no more.'

Mary Anne nodded.

This was indeed a dream, but Mary Anne saw Kat in the daylight as well as the night-time. Not that there was much daylight in the cell – only broken shafts in shadowy stripes on the dirt floor. They said Mary Anne was a spirit-child, that she had the 'gift', but it seemed only a curse to me. She spoke of no other ghosts, though, if they exist at all, there can be no shortage of spectres in Newgate. When

Kat appeared to her, the poor child retched at the smell of burning flesh until she vomited up her meagre ration. And I swear, whenever I sat close to Mary Anne, I could smell smoke in the dishevelled nest of her hair.

Unlike the others, I wasn't there when Kat met her end. I was in Newgate only six weeks before we left for Portsmouth; others had been there for a year or more, waiting for the next transport. And during that year, Kat had been put to the flames like a witch; although her crime was not murder, but the counterfeit of coins. She'd been led to the pyre past the hanging corpse of her husband in the yard. As a man, he'd suffered a kinder death. As a woman with the gall to fake the King's shilling, Kat was deemed to deserve a harsher punishment.

'She loved that *eejit*,' Kezia said when she told me the story. 'And look how she paid the price for his crimes.'

It was said that the executioner had taken pity on Kat, had strangled her quickly before setting the torch onto the faggots. Poor Kat was the very last woman to be burned. Afterwards, it was always the noose or the transport. Sometimes women had the choice. Sometimes they chose the noose.

For me, the crime was a common one: the snatch, on a whim, of a length of sprigged muslin. The punishment was seven years in Botany Bay and my journey hence was about to begin. What kind of land was it, that lay beyond the seas? Would I even survive the six-month voyage to get there? And how would I ever get back again?

The day of our departure dawned. We were to be the Second Fleet, and it was only two years since the First had set sail, so no convicts had returned to tell their stories. Some of the women had husbands and children they might never see again. I thought of my mother back in Ireland.

She was probably dead already, for the cough had all but consumed her the last time I'd been home. I wished I could cry at the thought of a family left behind. My dry eyes hurt more than tears.

Leaving the prison, squinting in unfamiliar winter sunshine, we were shackled, one to another, and squashed into and on top of a convoy of three coaches. We were to be released from the irons a few at a time under supervision at the various inns where we stopped on the way, for stop we must. The horses needed relief, as indeed we did ourselves. A shared piss pot does not do in a rolling coach.

For the first leg, as far as the White Horse in Cobham, I pushed myself into a seat inside. I didn't want to face the jeering as we crossed the busy London streets. Kezia, ever defiant, took a seat on top where she could curse the people who stopped to stare and spit on them as we passed; a last gesture to the country we were leaving behind.

'Look! It's Elizabeth, waving goodbye at the gates,' said Hannah as we set off. She pointed to a young woman in a red cloak, tresses of golden hair escaping from the hood.

'Elizabeth?'

'Ah, I forget how new you are, Bridge. She was one of us – though English, not Irish – but they pardoned her on account of her beauty. She is lovely, mind. Eyes the colour of cornflowers. They said she must be preserved for "home cultivation".' Hannah pulled a face. ''Tis a pity we were not all born so comely, eh Bridge?'

I bridled a little, having always thought myself comely enough, though we must have seemed a motley crew then, dressed in rags, hair unkempt. I'd grown used to the foul smell of unwashed bodies, but I saw the coachman recoil as we piled in, clutching our few belongings, dresses stained with sweat and food and leaks of monthly blood. It was the first time I'd been outside in the London streets since that fateful day.

Mrs Coles had said I could take the Monday morning off.
She was taking the children to her sister's, where there were
cousins to play with and where a second nursemaid would
have no function but to gossip with the resident one – and
there were many things Mrs Coles didn't want her sister to
know.

'She's a soft spot for you,' said Tabitha. 'A housemaid
never gets such privileges.' It was true. The pay was poor,
but the children were no longer babes that needed napkin
changes and feeding through the night, so when Tabitha
rose from her bed in our shared quarters before dawn to
make up the fires, I could turn over for a few precious extra
minutes.

Tabitha was no beauty, that's for sure, but at Sunday
church, she turned out in the prettiest pink gown I'd ever
seen... except those in Mrs Coles' boudoir, of course. I sat
beside her in the pew and stroked the delicate fabric of her
skirts while the droning voice of the priest wafted over me.

'How could you afford the cloth?' I whispered.

'I couldn't, you silly girl. I stole it.'

I was a little shocked. Tabitha was more enterprising
than her blank fish face implied.

'How?'

'The old trick. You ask to see several muslins in the light
by the window, wait until the assistant is distracted by
another customer, then shove the one you want under your
petticoats...'

'Let us pray,' said the priest. We knelt and recited our
prayers like good little Catholic girls, but I kept opening my
eyes and glancing at that pink dress. It was so very pretty.

We sat back on the hard wood of the pews. Tabitha
continued. 'Choose carefully though – enough for a gown,

not so much that you can't walk straight with the bolt between the legs of your drawers. Why don't you do it tomorrow, now that you've the morning off? Try Nobles on Tavistock Street. There's a new man in there, one of those ex-soldiers wounded in the American wars. Patch on his eye, and a limp – that'll make him slow.'

No, I told myself. Not theft. You're far too much of a coward, Bridget O'Reilly. As we filed out of the church, I asked Our Lady to keep me from such temptations. But she wasn't listening.

On that fateful morning off, I stood by the window of Nobles, staring through the mullioned glass at the most beautiful muslin I'd ever seen, pure white with sprigs of yellow flowers, and I just knew I had to have it. Sadly, the shop assistant was neither so blind nor so lame as Tabitha had implied, and the bolt of muslin was tightly bound and much heavier than I'd imagined. He knew my trick, he told the Bow Street Runner when his colleague had fetched him, by the 'bad walk' I made in trying to reach the door, 'like she'd a rod stuck up her fundament'.

Of course, I lost my place immediately and was dragged next day to the Bailey. I shouldn't have expected anything less – some of the women in Newgate stole only ribbon and met the same fate as mine – but when the judge uttered those words, 'lands across the seas,' etc., I almost fainted from the shock.

Portsmouth was a hive of activity. Most of the convicts on board were men, who were to spend almost all the journey in irons, while we women – if we behaved ourselves – would have the run of the ship. Something to be grateful for. But I'd travelled across the sea before, from Ireland, on a tranquil summer day, and even then, the swell of the waves had brought on the nausea.

'They say you get used to it,' said Hannah.

The ship was called The Neptune. It was the largest of the fleet and was to carry hundreds of us. Aboard the vessel, the soldiers of the New South Wales Regiment in charge of us took away our few things, any little combs and pins, and bid us, in turn, take a cold bath in wooden troughs set up for the purpose. 'Decontamination,' they called it. I shivered in the dirty water, conscious of the grinning sailors contorting themselves into knots to try to catch a glimpse.

We were presented with a 'dress'; a shapeless sack of rough canvas.

'Lice-free,' said a soldier, as he thrust the garment into my arms. 'We want no bloody *vermin* on board.' He spat the word at me. *Vermin*. Dregs from the bottom of life's barrel. Though all that stood between the dainty nursemaid, taking Gussie and Lydia Coles for a walk through a leafy park, and this convict woman that I'd become, was that one stupid mistake. After the 'bath', we were lined up on deck for inspection.

Even after the weeks of degradation in Newgate, that 'inspection' was the lowest point. The officers passed along the line, appraising us. It took a moment for me to realise what was happening, as they pushed aside the old women, the ugly, the pockmarked.

'For God's sake, smile!' Hannah whispered to me.

'Why?'

'They're picking mistresses, for the voyage.'

'Why would I want to be someone's mistress?'

'How innocent you are, Bridge,' she said. 'For privileges, of course. Better food, a comfortable bed, less disgusting jobs... We'll be months aboard. Better make the best of it.'

I looked at the men as they passed, many middle-aged, balding. They would have wives and children at home. Indeed, one of them – who admittedly was not partaking in this 'parade' – a haughty-looking lieutenant, had his young wife with him, and his child. She'd a comely face, the wife, but it was spoiled by a sour expression whenever she dropped the scarf from her nose. Not that I blamed her for her reluctance to breathe the air – the miasma onboard was suffocating; a mingle of foul stinks rising from the bilge deck, made more pungent still by the buckets of excrement tossed overboard.

Mary Anne stood beside me in the line. Her slight body pressed against mine, and I could feel her trembles. An officer passed by and lifted her chin.

'What's your name?'

'Mary Anne, Sir.'

'How old are you, child?'

'Thirteen.'

I saw his eyes registering this fact. Was that expression one of sympathy for her condition? Or did I see him lick the inside of his lip?

'An innocent still, I'll bet,' he said.

Mary Anne said nothing.

I couldn't bear it. She'd suffered so much. And all she'd done to receive this sentence was steal a sack of potatoes out of sheer, desperate hunger. I didn't know whether he would try to take her for his 'little girl', but I had to speak out. 'She's a child, Sir... Just a child,' I piped up. 'She knows nothing of the ways of the world.'

'And you are...?'

'Bridget O'Reilly, Sir.'

'Bridget... Are you saying you *do* know "the ways of the world"?'

'No, Sir, but I'm nineteen. And Mary Anne is so small, and so afraid...'

The officer looked me up and down.

'Well then, I think you'll do for now, Bridget O'Reilly.

Come to my cabin after supper tonight. Do you
understand?'

I nodded.

His first name was Valentine, he said later. The patron
saint of love. What love could there be in such a situation,
with such a man? But I was no virgin. I'd lain with a man
before – well, a boy, in truth – several times on the banks
of the Shannon. And this Valentine was not a violent
man. Lying against him in his cabin afterwards, smelling
the brandy on his breath, I felt a strange sense of self-
command. I'd had no choice, and yet a part of me felt in
control because I'd deflected him from Mary Anne. I'd done
a good thing.

The next morning, more men were brought from the hulks
and loaded into the caged sections of the orlop. I'd seen
the conditions on that deck. The men were shackled by the
wrists and ankles and chained to another convict. For once,
I thanked fate that I was a woman, allowed to breathe fresh
air and see the outside world, for all that it would soon
consist of nothing but water and horizon.

'See the old man with the stick?' said Hannah, pointing
to a moving heap of clothes hanging on a form that barely
looked human, so thin was it. 'I knew of him in Newgate.
He swore he'd never see Botany Bay and thrust a lancet
into each of his eyes because he thought they'd never
transport a blind man... Yet here he is.'

On the deck, I found Kezia tattooing Mary Anne's
forearm with a sewing needle and charcoal diluted with
spittle for the dye. The child was biting down on her bottom
lip, tears running down her face.

'What are you doing that for?' I asked.

'I'm giving her a swallow.'

'But you're hurting her...'

'She wants it.'

'Bridge, you must get one too,' said Mary Anne. 'If we die, the swallow will carry our souls to the gates of heaven.'

I shook my head.

Kezia beckoned me towards her and whispered into my ear. 'She won't last the voyage. We must give her some hope.'

That final night, we sat on deck draping the shawls we'd been issued over our heads against the night's frost. The moon was full, bright silver. We could see the harbour lights from our anchorage. We could hear music coming from the taverns, taste the fried fish in the air, smell the tar on a hundred masts that creaked as they bobbed on the swells. I tried to hold it all inside my mind. I thought about the open ocean that lay ahead, when the night would bring only stars and storms; and beyond, to Botany Bay, where the darkness would echo with the calls of strange creatures and the war cries of natives with torches and spears.

Mary Anne leaned in against Kezia for warmth.

'Say goodbye to all this, little one,' said Kezia. 'To this miserable fucking country. It'll be a new start for you, you'll see. You'll be grand.'

Mary Anne smiled, but I could see the skull inside her face. Her arms were thin and brittle, like chicken wishbones. Kezia was right – she wouldn't survive the voyage.

Then Kezia began to sing The Lament, her voice deep and velvety. Many of us knew the words from our own mothers' knees, and one by one, we joined in. I felt the women's arms tighten around my shoulders, and in that moment, I loved them, I really did. For sure, it was an Irish song, but strangely, it was not nostalgia that swept through me then. Not sadness even. No, it was a kind of... Pride. We were explorers, going into the unknown. It would be hard, and friends would die on the voyage. Perhaps I would die myself, but I would die trying.

That was the last night I ever saw the Old World. 158 convicts were to die on that voyage. The swallow carried away Mary Anne's beautiful soul after six long weeks. We watched the sailors slide her body so easily into the water, weighing no more than the small sack of potatoes that had brought her there. Those months were the hardest of my life. But what I didn't know then was that this would not always be a punishment; that, one day, I would be free and would discover a land that was, oh yes, harsh and pestilent and unforgiving, and yet so beautiful, so wild and vast, a land of sweeping sandy bays and blue mountains. I didn't know that, one day, I would work my own farm, breed my own sheep, till my own land; that I would find the love of my life and bear a child who would be proud to call himself 'Australian'. I didn't know then that nobodies, convict women, 'vermin', would turn out to be the Mothers of a Nation.

Roof of the World

Laila Lock

A mere bus ride away
The gulls are shrieking bedlam at dark nimbus
Razor clams, Chubb locked for the season
Are lifted by dark surges far beyond the dry line
Landing as silent relatives to alien, conical hats.
Behind a sea wall the prom woman is prepositioned,
Countering updrafts with inverted umbrella
Like a wrong-sided magnet.
A diorama as distant as a bus ride to the moon.

I had listened to the sluicing of the cars,
The dirty rain, becoming frozen in 4'6.

The only way is up.
I follow curlicues as if artex could become art.
Hokusai's tendril hands raising foamy hopes;
The ziggurat lines of the plasterer
Mercurial sledge runs away from the cold
To approximate lagoon Picasso Blue G142
Tumbling into surf the white noise fore-fronted.
And then,
I blow the conch,
Charge shorelines with the bad 'Flies' boys,
Shin the hairy boughs,
Snuff up jungly mulch, grasp overripe fruits
Plunge toes in forever coral
Knowing particles, every grain.
The obliterating glare of a south sea orb
Gives incentive to see.

Footstep on the stair
I wind back around the bulb of a distant sun's
Tropical fast descent – the lashed curtain.
It's become dark.
The peripheral book on the cabinet
Explains for Boucher
At The Setting of The Sun you will drag darkness.
Forget to
Wake

"You were far away for a minute there,"
He says, holding my hand.
But because of those sad eyes
I fail to tell him about the sea.

The Tooth Fairy

Petra Lindnerova

She sent me teeth in the post again. She was overly
protective, my mother. Every time a girl died, she would
send a couple – small milky beads that rattled like
keys between fingers. They were always clean, slightly
misshapen, like the gravel lining rich people's driveways
in Primrose Hill. No weedy roots, no dried gunk. I could
imagine her scooping up the minuscule gemstones while a
child sat teary-eyed and snotty in the dentist seat, the sharp
light making the upset gums shine in deep pink.

She always told me I was not careful enough. When
walking the streets, crossing the road, talking to strangers.
And because she lived so far away, the news about girls –
reduced to bluish, swollen bodies – always arrived days
later.

'Why didn't you tell me the news?' she said on the other
end.

'It's not news, Mum.'

She could get very distraught at that. Why would I stay
in such a dangerous, sly city where one could not go for a
walk, a jog, a run? Did I want her to lose sleep every night
that I forgot to type good night to her? Her next-door
neighbour would sit on her right, vigorously nodding,
telling me to come home. Where it's safe. She always took
part in our video calls because she frequented my mother's
house more than her own, avoiding her husband.

'You can walk the streets at any time here!' she said.

'You need to start taking this more seriously,' Mum
added.

Then the mail started coming, tiny glass jars that

resembled lab vials. It freaked me out at first, but I could not quite bear to throw them away. I would dream of kids with large gaps in their mouths at night, slurring and lisping through math classes. Just like the ones I taught. Arguing with their peers over the last cookie they could barely chew, chocolate chips stuck in the holes like bugs. Mum always gave them a reward for their bravery – a shiny plastic ring for the girls, a pencil with a tooth-shaped eraser for the boys. They would flaunt these treasures at school the next day, completely forgetting their missing teeth.

Some of the parents, of course, wanted to keep them. Put them in a velvet box like dainty jewellery and then show their offspring ten years later, like a badge of honour for forced growing up. They forgot they were former children themselves and that this ritualistic hoarding used to make their eyes roll. That they had been disgusted with the decade-old deciduous carcasses presented on a pedestal. The teeth were supposed to be temporary. But there they were, boxed up and treasured and oftentimes handled for show even though nobody asked.

I started putting labels on the jars. There was Kate, Romana, Becky, Aisling, Ameera... It became a calendar, lined in a perfect row on my shelf. I'd put my books on the floor to make room. After each third jar, I would go visit home to calm Mum's nerves. Took a bus to Liverpool Street at 3.00 am, then a train to the airport, then the flight. I told myself I'd consider moving once I had a full jaw.

I lived in a small studio space painted dark blue. If I ever lit a candle, the walls gained a shimmery quality that made them look like they were closing in, yet never fully compressed me into a squash of meat and bones. I would almost exclusively eat soup and bread because the heating never worked properly, but in that small space, a boiling pot would fix the problem immediately. I looked too thin and didn't like myself, but at least I was warm. I speed-walked everywhere to make sure the blood in my body was hot and pumping. The pupils called me Miss Tiny behind my back, which was too small to serve as a barrier between gossip and its target. Generally, though, they liked me. Most of them lived in the same estate building I did, and sometimes I could hear their parents shouting at them to do their homework. Behaving well was compulsory because their mum or dad would never take their side if they got in trouble. That only happened in affluent families where teachers were the subservient creatures, catering knowledge to the pampered kids who know if they do poorly, money comes to the rescue to balance out.

The latest jar was called Samantha. A teacher just like me, with nervous creases around her eyes and a low-cut fringe. The early winter sunset had betrayed her on the way from work just off Battersea station. Too many notebooks in her hands prevented her from punching or scratching the man. The news anchor threw away a stinging comment about her black huggy skirt, the same one I wore as part of my uniform. An ugly, thick material reaching all the way below the knees. Nobody mentioned that. As she did with every personal link, Mum kept reminding me of Samantha's occupation over the phone, saying smart girls were the ultimate bait for psychos. I told her to stop using the derogative word, and she replied I was focusing on the wrong thing again.

'See? Evidently, I'm not smart. No need to worry.'

I would mock her for her assumptions and misconceptions until she and the neighbour both scoffed like two disconcerted mares. The neighbour's eyes were so puffy, I could barely discern where the eyelid ended. I cancelled the call hastily, both because I was about to go to a march and because I could not look at the inflamed capillaries spider webbing her pupils. I sent a private text to Mum to talk sense into her friend.

'She needs to ditch him like you did.'

People marched slowly, which aggravated me. This being my first time, I was unused to the reasonable pace conducive to slogan shouting and sign-waving. I kept stepping on heels and crashing into backs like a drunk, but the crowd's density warmed me up. I could try and slow down. I joined in to scream the names. They were all over the signs like subtitles, forming into heavy pebbles in my mouth. The girls in my class shared many of them. The more I said them, the more my mouth watered and my tongue slipped. Under the sticky dampness of my raincoat, I felt saturated. With unfairness and fear that tasted like gritty salt. I was crying, but nobody saw because of the rain. In a way, every face was washed over by a waterfall.

I wanted to break into a run but was trapped by masses of moving bodies, strained ribcages. The chanting filled my ears. I thought of numbers on the blackboard and multiplications. Started devising random problems to solve, potential questions to put on the text pop quiz. But I quickly slipped. *Kate, Romana, Becky, Aisling, Ameera and Samantha are hanging out in the park. It's 5.00 pm, and they need to be home by 6.00 pm. Their journeys home are less than half an hour each. If they take no shortcuts, keep to the pavement and don't put their earphones in, how come none of them ever makes it home?*

'But Miss, this doesn't make sense. There is no formula to calculate this.'

I forced myself through the soggy crowd. Most people failed to register the panic in my eyes and mumbled swear words at me. Or maybe I was imagining it, still dazed from this mosh pit of sadness. Once I got to the deserted side street, the noise faded and my jaw unclenched. The pressure had turned my teeth soft and malleable like clay. As I stood there, opening and closing my mouth, I could see the big block of protesters going by, an endless rippling curtain of coats and cloaks. I goggled dumbly, listening to the cartilage popping each time I opened just to shut with a blunt click. Like a fish out of water.

I shuddered all the way to my flat, missing the heat of the crowd but terrified from its intensity. A group of rowdy young boys on the bus was talking about what they were getting their girlfriends for Christmas. Laughter erupted when one of them gestured at his crotch.

'This one needs no wrapping, you get me?!'

I was seething, half due to the cold, half due to the appalling comment. They noticed and started speaking louder, leaning their enormous bums on the railing in front of my seat. I held my backpack on my knees to block out the view. When the bus chucked me out in front of the green, and the doors closed in front of them, I sighed loudly. It sped off, their leery faces now a memory. My legs did not seem to work, and I had to walk across at a snail pace, murmuring names to myself like a necromancer. Once sprawled on the bed, I fell straight to sleep, the wet rag of my clothes the only blanket. The walls seemed mere inches from my face.

There were countless messages. She thought I had got trampled during that march, flattened to one with the road. She kept firing scenarios at me, livelier and more inventive than any of my pupils' excuses. I had simply fallen asleep, my phone on silent in the depths of my pocket. I over-explained myself in a voice muted and rough by the cold resulting from spending the night in a soaked bundle. A person-sized wet patch was imprinted on the bedsheet, the navy dimness of the studio like an underwater crime scene.

I had not managed to strip the mattress before leaving for work. It was late, and I was unable to rush, tip-tapping as if an invisible hand held me on a leash. Mum demanded to see my face on video, probably to make sure I truly regretted neglecting my texting duties.

'You look pale,' she said.

For the first time in months, her face was the only one in the frame. I ignored her comment and asked about the neighbour.

'I am sure she will be over later. We are baking a cocoa cake.'

I looked around, the daylight so blinding it made the post-rain pavement glow. It squeaked under my shoes as I trod along.

'Anyway, you're focusing on the wrong thing again.'

After a sharp inhale of petrichor, I lied I was close to the school and needed to head inside. She let me go. She later sent a picture of the cake, tall and spongy with creamy frosting. I looked at it as I waited for a class to file in, a girl swishing by me remarking sugar is bad for the teeth. She smiled ear to ear, revealing one black hole punctuated by a couple chipped pearls. So proud of them, she and her pigtailed group, dying to keep them white and intact. Meanwhile, the boys wanted theirs all gone already, biting into hard radioactively green apples in the hope they stay stuck in the flesh. They wanted the sharp grownup incisors, molars to grind aggressively. I gave them problems to solve independently and stared out the window until the end of the lesson; at the trees swaying in the wind, the tips swishing back and forth. The streets were empty, rubbish gliding across the road – the modern-day tumbleweed. I dreaded the sound of the bell, knowing I'd be expunged into the wild with this newfound fright in my legs.

I stopped turning the radio on. Ignored the newspapers.

Overboiled the soup so often the alarm became a continuous siren in my mind. I was one jar away from booking flight tickets, the calendar now populated with names. I didn't go to another march or vigil or memorial service. They always happened far away, in pastel-coloured parts of London where policemen were trusted, where people were most worried about their plump pooches being stolen. They burnt saccharine fragrance sticks while marching. I could not sit on another bus. I largely ignored my mother in fear of unveiling what had become of me. She succeeded – I was scared. Eventually, she stopped calling.

A woman from the estate knocked on my door to complain when I woke up the whole neighbourhood with another batch of soup at seven in the morning. She bit her tongue numerous times, almost addressing me as Miss Tiny – her daughter was in my class. I apologised for the disruption and blamed it on a faulty sensor. I would get it looked into as soon as possible. There was barely any smoke in the place, truly. But she was not listening. Her eyes were firmly planted behind me, widening every second until they bulged out as if she had been shot. I half expected to see a trickle of blood escape her mouth. With the door ajar, my calendar was on display in all its disturbing glory, like a cohort of victims, with their names in block capitals, their teeth bare and glinting. She forgot about the noise that so bothered her, and her face clicked back from shock to horrified awareness. I could neither explain nor catch up with her retreating figure.

To subdue my full-blown paranoia, I tried to break a sweat in the park. I felt crazier with each attempt, limping around the green and swearing at my legs. At school, the kids stopped smiling at me and whispered to each other.

'Miss Tiny is a witch.'

'I heard she can pull your teeth out with a blink.'

I did not argue. There was a well-written formal notice in my desk drawer. It was only a matter of time.

The package arrived without the usual preliminary phone call full of reproach. Out of touch with the news, I finally gave in. With no control over my shaking fingers, I opened the website on my phone to find the name for my last label. Tears were pouring down my face, my throat lumping up. I wanted to shout at my mother, tell her she won. But I could find no relevant headline. I scoured through all social media, ate up heaps of unnecessary threads of spite and angst, watched even the least trusty broadcasts. Nothing. I resorted to calling Mum. She did not blame me. She cried. She had baked that cake on her own that day.

I travelled back for the funeral, arriving just before the service. Her husband was in the front row looking devastated, hands clasped religiously like God himself was going to attend to condole him. My mother stared at the crown of his head as she muttered her prayers as if casting a curse on him.

'You were focusing on the wrong thing,' I whispered.

Asylum

Anna Seidel

Crossing my lips, you trace each crest, crease, bend,
the branch jabbed soles of my bifid tongue,
feel thin mountain air sped breath-beats;

Explore raw paths plied in soil, riptides of my mouth,
where prayers of poison, prayers of thorns
near childhood dreams rest;

Where secret thoughts silently take seed,
cradling lost roots on taste buds,
hiding a grief finely sewn into flesh.

Did you find the words that had flout borders,
smuggled in the cavities of my wisdom teeth, tunnels
through which memory haunts my mind
like an endless reverberating tremor?
Did you ever have to measure a word's ballast?

These exiled idioms held so much for so long.
Wrapped in sheepskin, vowels brimming,
their lettered backs broken from all the weight.

In each cavern of a kiss, I search foreign words
to re-sculpt my story from, seek harbor
in strange tongues, that so often fail to hold.

Fires that Burn Away the Light

Naomi Elster

The salty smell of cured pork brings a new headiness to the twisting streets of the *judería*. This entire city was built like a nest of snakes, streets thin and twisting, to shield its people from heat and to disorient their enemies. But in the Jewish quarter especially, there are too many shadows. Houses lean in so close overhead they almost seem to touch. The walls are too high and when you lose yourself in these twisting, turning, churning streets, you imagine those walls creeping closer to trap and choke you. *Maybe our ancestors consented to have them here only if they could be crammed into this tight corner, out of sight*, Ana thinks. *But at least it is easy to pass unseen.* She stops, her eyes confronting a row of homes born into a faith that abhors pork, now like butchers plying for trade, with large joints of *jamón* hung prominently in windows and door frames.

'*Será suficiente*?' she asks her mentor and companion. 'Will it be enough?' Mari doesn't answer, and Ana wonders if it's because she can't, or because she won't. Not yet.

Once out of the city, they travel east with speed, hoping that they are still unnoticed. The lands are all so dry: the fertile plains around the rivers run along like veins through the yellow fields and red dust.

'The Guadalquivir,' Mari murmurs, as they follow its path. 'Its name from the Arabic – I wonder for how much longer we will still call it that?'

They reach the place where the Guadalquivir meets the Genil, where they can scry both rivers at once. And in the water, they see fire and blood.

In the Genil, a red sun rises over the snow of the Sierra Nevada, brushing colour into the rich sandstone of the Alhambra. The long and tall blocks of the Alcazaba – that stocky fortress, all crude strength and no charm. Its strength has failed. A yellow and red flag flutters over its tower, bodies are scattered like litter on all sides as the hill of La Sabika winds down to the city. Men's lives thrown away like rubbish. Women, soon to be forgotten, waiting to find out who they belong to now.

In the wide, sluggish waters of the Guadalquivir, no other war was flowing towards them. Not another enemy from the outside. But there are flames. Angry, treacherous flames. Black stains on their white buildings, black stains on the honour of the city, which their descendants will never whitewash out.

Ana is always the first to speak, the quickest to act, even when she knows she shouldn't.

'How long before Seville knows that Granada has fallen? And Mari, the flames? What are they?'

When they get back, Auxi, the youngest novice and the first given to Ana to mentor, is washing a body. '*La tardanza*,' she says, without looking up.

La tardanza. The delay. *La tardanza* is snatching away more and more lives. *Sevillanos* now only bring their sick to the *curanderas* by night. In the dark, the pounding of the brass ring on the thick wood door alternates with hoarse, desperate whispers. The desperate sound and the fearful silence as two fears battle in the families of the ill: fear of diseases of the body rampaging through their loved ones, and fear of the disease of the soul of this city as it rampages ever more desperately for heretics. The new rulers don't like the *curanderas*. They think these women are not fearful enough, and so they are not to be trusted, and now citizens fear being associated with them. Fear breeds delay, which allows diseases to take root so deeply in a body that the most skilled healers can no longer pull them out.

Auxi tenderly folds the young girl's hands, smooths back her hair from the stiffening face. Auxi has in her the kind of strength that yields acts of love and kindness long after others would have said there was little point. But she is as trusting as she is trustworthy, and in these treacherous times, Ana fears for her.

There is little to do. The sun should still be some months away from its most pitiless, but all of their days are as hot and dead as the very depths of summer. The light pounds the patio and pushes back out in all four directions against the cloisters' shade, stretching from cobbles onto flagstones, banishing shadow even from the walls. No respite. They are too unsettled to sleep. The women worry about the water, and about the witch-hunts to come. They hide from the sun in blue and white mosaic rooms, which should house healing patients, or under the shade of the orange tree where they used to teach eager students. The only sound is the click of fans. They can do little now but move the heat around, but at least wrists still have purpose.

Despite the heat, Mari walks without shoes, letting her feet feel the soapy terracotta and the rough cobbles. Her fingers travel over the whitewashed plaster, trail through the fountain, trace the patterns on the mudejar tiles. She is trying to remember every detail, every sight, sound, touch. She never thought there might be a time that this was no longer before her eyes, but the visions are clear: she must find a way to leave. If she escapes, she will go north to hide between walls of stone and behind veils of rain. If she does not leave on time, it's not just that she will die, it's that all of their skills, honed over centuries, will be lost forever.

Only Ana knows what Mari is beginning to plan. Ana has seen why it is necessary. She has seen it happen somewhere else. A series of dreams set in a deep green land, a land where smoke rises from the charcoal ground, where ravines cut deep gashes into dark, dense forests. She saw a people, shorter than Europeans and skin the colour of milky coffee. She saw the vivid colours of their flowing blouses and belted skirts, and intuited the wisdom and knowledge of the advanced society they have built. And then she saw them die, from the blades and from the diseases of trespassers. Helpless in sleep, she watched as all their records, all the books they used to preserve their wisdom, burned on bonfires lit by Spanish soldiers.

Madness murders reason, lights flames that will burn away the light and take the world into dark days. They must find a way to survive, to preserve, to persevere.

But for now, she needs to absorb the essence of her home, so that there is something she can take with her. See how the patio is a perfect square? All life comes from water: maybe that's why everything is centred around the small stone fountain. See how those arches loop gracefully one after the other, dancing around the whole patio and stretching to support the next floor? See the white walls to deflect the sun's glare, the brown tiles, baked once in the kiln to prepare them, and now baked again where they lie under that sun?

Then came the day that Auxi went out, and did not come back. An *auto-da-fe* is called only when there are enough prisoners to justify the spectacle. They are becoming more frequent, and the women did not have to wait long before the next appointed day. They almost never go beyond their doors now, so they stand shoulder-to-shoulder on the patio. They keep their own silent vigil as the unfamiliar language and rhythm of the night prayers murmur to a close. As a murky day sets in, they look to the smoke, and listen for her screams.

'Could she... Is it possible...?'

'She's small, and quick. She could have slipped away...'

'She cared for many people with enough gold to spare her.'

'But then why has she not come back to us?'

'Well... *La Merced.*'

La Merced. The mercy. It's what they nickname it, when the wealthy condemned or their families pay to be taken out of the line and strangled, to be dead before the pyres are lit.

'Or maybe flames mutilate our voices so that not even our friends recognise it.'

Ana knows she should have kept this thought to herself, but she is out of hope.

The next time, the *curanderas* gathered to listen again. There was something new in the screams, something which curdled the blood like never before. Ana threw a hood over her face and slipped past the gate. The healers waited, silent, until Ana returned, but she gave no news. Some thought she would never speak again until the third night she walked the corridors, her feet slapping against cold stones, and they heard her repeated whisper to the night shadows.

'Children. They are burning children now.'

The fires stoke higher and higher. The screams get louder, but the streets more silent. Ana says that the only honesty left is in the screams of the condemned.

She cannot stay behind those walls. She walks to El Prado, where the trees still let their leaves and flowers float down to the gentle yellow ground. But their delicate purple flowers are crushed beneath the weight of the *quemadero* platform. She sees new statues being built. For the first time in over 700 years, there is no king but theirs, and they say all must bow down before this version of holiness. Yet

they are chiselling out hard white statues that show saints
and angels bowing down in front of royalty and riches. Men
on pulpits proclaim one true faith as ropes cut into wrists
and ankles and pull bodies apart. The buildings are still so
very white, even as the city burns its very humanity.

Street signs, which preserved the names of the great
learners and teachers of the Cordóba caliphate, are being
taken down. Ana sees a new sign for Calle Isabel la Catolica.
The name of Queen Isabella carries so much weight.
But this world has become so afraid of women that Ana
wonders how much power she really has.

Mari is standing across the threshold, one foot on the
cobbles of this outer courtyard, one hand against the hot
white stone there, the other hand and foot inside, on the
cloister flagstones, the cool tiles still decorated in the
Moroccan style.

'What do you feel?' Ana asks.

Mari rests her forehead on the doorframe. 'Our home has
memories, and they confirm my suspicions. There never
was a time we had to seal both doors, until now.'

'Mari, you are the only one of us powerful enough to look
down through time. What do you see?'

'Scars. Lasting scars of this time, even when all this land
exists as one nation. I've seen this new, unified country
run warm and run a fever. Our descendants will remain
capable of great kindness and barbaric brutality. In its kind
periods, the people won't stare down the other histories
they have endured, and so, the hot bloodlust we see now
will always be here, simmering beneath the soil and latent
within the veins of our people. I have seen our sailors
return victorious with great treasures they have plundered
from faraway lands, king settled, and I have seen our rulers
and merchants ask no questions as to how those gains were
gotten from lands they say had no people.'

Ana thought again of her dreams, of the thickly forested lands, the sickness, the swords, and the bonfire.

'I have seen the songs of the gipsies celebrated by those who persecute them. Even when we no longer flock to the *autos-da-fe*, men in glittering dress will still drive darts and lances into flesh for show and for sport and call it sophistication. All this great land's nuances, complexities and intrigues reduced to *machísmo* clichés of blood and sand.'

They stepped inside, bolting the door.

'You speak as though there's little hope.'

'The world will come out of this shadow. The future could bring us advances not even I can see. But we must find a way to reach that future.'

'I went through the *judería* today.'

'She is not there.'

'That's not what I meant. The *jamón*... It's given me an idea.'

The women are glad to have something to do, and piece by piece, Ana's idea takes form and grows. They use their redundant bandages to sew costumes, robes and hoods that hide the size and shape of their bodies, because the new fashion fears individuality. They build great statues, and platforms to hold them. They open their gates again and spread word of their plans.

Now, *Sevillanos* without the means to flee the city flock to the *curanderas* instead, who find themselves needing to stage more and more parades to accommodate all those desperate for a visible show of devotion to exonerate themselves from the suspicion, which now falls so easily, like a loose blade. Before long, they have extended the festival to the entire week leading up to the sacred Friday of death. The Marquis himself sends a gift of fine purple drapes.

'The colour of royalty for the king and queen of heaven,' the messenger says. The real meaning is that the inquisitors answer to no one; even royalty fear the tribunals.

Ana paints tears onto statues of the Virgin Mary, hoping that it will slake some of the mob's thirst to see women suffer.

Mari starts to quietly, carefully plan the parades, devising combinations of costumes, theatrics, and routes which will allow those most in danger to slip away, to disappear from the city like ghosts.

The week arrives. Hot, heady streets are drowned in funerary incense as wax drips onto cobblestones and the bare feet burning upon them. A drum beat, solemn and loud, and trumpets to announce their presence. The men no longer walk proudly beneath the platforms, but instead sway and stagger, so the eerie statues undulate side-to-side, taking on a new, menacing drama. No faces are visible beneath those hoods. An army of black hooded ghosts is on a solemn march, evoking the very spirit of death and despair that the marchers now know so well.

These are women who have always been free. Now they wear the mask of the oppressed and of the oppressor at once. But they are only masks, a way to hide in plain sight.

'This long storm will pass,' Mari tells them. 'When the world leaves this shadow, we can cast our hoods off and everything we have worked for will still be there.'

Ana thinks of it differently. She is determined to outsmart them, to be the witch they could not burn.

Breadcrumbs

Molly Smith Main

She looked down at the blank screen with its cursor flashing anxiously in dismay. What did she want to say? 'Help, I'm so lonely!' sounded a little dramatic, and although honest, it didn't seem quite positive enough to make any friends. She scrolled down slowly, pressing the tiny heart-shaped button robotically. Photo after photo of beautifully drawn eyebrows arched over thickly lashed eyes looking away from her and towards some perfect life.

Search #womensfashion

Glancing down at her worn leggings, she unhelpfully smudged a stray speck of tomato soup down her leg. 'What can I say that is going to be even remotely interesting to anybody on here?' She'd had her clothes for ages, and every time she attempted to put on make-up, she ended up looking like a cheap drag artist. Her daughter had been the one who had suggested she create an Instagram account. Pearl posted a photo every day and said it would be a lovely way of seeing what the grandchildren were up to. It had taken her a while to get used to it – all these buttons and scrolling were slightly different from the typewriter she had learned on at school, but now she had the hang of it; she loved seeing their smiling faces and what they had been up to. She wished she could see more of them, but they lived so far away.

Search #missinggrandchildren

She frowned as she scrolled past a photo of a bowl of food, broccoli and sweetcorn, something black and some rice. She was still completely confused about why people thought it was remarkable that they had made some food. She tried to imagine collecting a fat packet of photographs from Boots, after anxiously waiting for a few days, only to be greeted by plates of beans on toast, bowls of cornflakes and a mug of tea.

Search #whydopeoplepostpicturesoffood?

Pearl had thought Instagram might help her make friends – friends in her phone as she called them – as she didn't get out much anymore, especially now. She had only spoken face to face with one person this week, and that was Will at the paper shop when she had run out of teabags. She couldn't remember when she'd become so isolated and introverted? Perhaps when she had left the factory four years ago after over 30 years of service – she missed her colleagues there, missed their chats in the tea-room and the feeling of camaraderie as they put on their aprons and hairnets and trooped into the 'oven' as they called it. Dr Jacob had suggested she 'get out more'. But where was she to go?

Search #getoutmore

It was 11.00 am, time for her morning mug of tea. This Instagram could take up the whole morning if she let it. She sat at her kitchen table, looking out the window at the trees at the bottom of her garden. Her Dad had planted that apple tree before her elder brothers and her were born. They had loved eating the apples and climbing in the branches if their mum wasn't looking.

After lunch finished at 1.00 pm sharp, she put on the radio, pulled her apron over her head, and began making her bread. She had always loved the smell of fresh bread ever since her father had come home from the bakery with a warm white loaf wrapped in crunchy brown paper. Her mum had coarsely sliced the loaf, and they would all sit around the kitchen table stuffing chunks of soft bread dripping with melting margarine into their hungry mouths. She tipped out the mix and began to push and fold, squash, and knead the warm, pliable dough. As she squished, she thought back to when her daughter was little, how she had played happily in the street, laughing loudly and crying for attention when she had fallen over or was hungry. She'd had to work hard at the time, juggling work and family but never realised just how lucky she was to have all her loved ones around her. She had adored being a mum, keeping her baby safe and warm, listening to her read and encouraging Pearl to keep learning. She had told her stories every night before bedtime. One of their favourite stories was Hansel and Gretel. She'd always thought Hansel was so clever to leave a little trail of breadcrumbs so they could find the way back. She smiled when she remembered her daughters' squeals of delight as she read about the witch in her cottage in the woods. She wondered now if the witch was just a lonely, old woman. Stuck in her house looking out at the trees, pleased for some young company and smiling faces.

Search #lonelywomen

Well, blimey, that was a search she wasn't going to try again.

She'd been ever so proud when her daughter had gone to university. She was the first person from the family to go, and her degree had meant she had been able to get a good job – it was just a shame she had moved so far away as she'd have loved to be able to help to look after the kids.

Search #grandma

Since she was no longer working, she had sorted through all her clothes and washed and mended the ones she wore. She scrolled once again through photos of glossy haired women, teeth so white they almost looked blue, wearing tiny, figure-hugging dresses and huge, towering heels clutching branded patent bags and enormous sunglasses as they jetted off to some exotic, luxury holiday. She'd been on holiday a few times but never left England. Her late husband hadn't wanted to travel, but they had saved up and gone to Bournemouth a few times. She had loved the feel of the sun and sand on her skin. They had stayed in a B&B looking over Boscombe Pier, somehow fish and chips tasted even better at the seaside. It had been three years now since he had gone. The house was too quiet without him.

Search #matureladiesfashion

Ah, that was a bit more like it – there were pictures of 'real' people, wearing 'normal' clothes. Also, a few interesting posts about women her age. Silver-haired ladies. Even a post about 'empowering women'. She wondered if she had ever been empowered. The famous Bread Shortages of 1977? She had stood outside the factory with her pal, Sue and all their workmates, waving their placards, striking for extra money. Sue had died last winter after suffering from throat cancer. They had all felt powerful when they returned to work and were given a few pounds extra in their wage packet. Felt rather daring now.

As she walked through the hall, she caught a glimpse of herself in the mirror. Her hair was a yellowing grey as she neared her 70th year. She had kept it long and usually wore it tied in a ponytail, just as she had when she was younger and had to keep it tucked in a net cap for the factory. The radio was playing a song by The Beatles, and she suddenly felt like a teenager again. She carefully hauled the loaf out of the oven and set it on a cooling rack. It was a thing of beauty. The golden crust glistened in the light from the window, and the smell was amazing. She decided to take a photo of it and send it to Pearl. The grandchildren had always loved her bread too. After a few attempts – one of which involved her getting a rather disturbing photo of herself with what looked like a huge chin – she got one she was happy with and sent it off to Pearl.

'Wow! Mum, that looks like a delicious loaf!! Jack and

Meg would love some of that! I'll post it on your Instagram page! #artisanbread – Take care, see you soon! P xxx'

The next morning, she switched her phone on. A little red circle was on her Instagram button. When she clicked on it, she saw the photo of her bread had over 836 likes. There were so many comments and questions, too –

This looks amazing!

How did you make this?

I wish I could do that!

Can I have the recipe?

You've inspired me to bake bread!

How did you get the crust so golden? Mine never looks like that!

And 127 people wanted to follow her – whatever that meant.

Breadcrumbs

The Stars are Falling

Sophie Evans

and we lie here watching it happen,
this astral Armageddon.

The constellations crumble piece by piece,
Andromeda, Cassiopeia, Ursas Minor and Major,
disintegrate into nothingness before our eyes.

The moon's crescent smile spits
specks of light down on us, and she grins
as though it is the greatest gift she should give.

Like pieces of glowing confetti,
the stars twirl and flutter towards the Earth, leaving
the endless night a pool of midnight ink; in this moment,
if the world were to tip upside down,
we'd drown in it.

Catch one for me, you whisper
and I stretch my hands to the heavens,
waiting, hoping, aching for
a star to descend in our direction. And then

minutes later, we spot one plummeting towards us.
You jump up, shouting *over there over there* and
I run towards the light, leap into the air,
and as my fist closes around it,
the damned thing burns a hole
through my palm and
falls to its final resting place

at our feet.

The night air stinks of my singed skin
and upon further inspection we discover
that the star I had tried to catch
was, in fact,
the Sun.

About the Authors

Aby Atilol
Aby Atilol is a product manager by day. Somehow, in her busy schedule, she finds time to write short stories. She recently completed an online short story course at City Lit.UK, and is more interested in the short story form than ever before.

Aisling Watters
Aisling Watters won the Novel London Award in 2020 and has been shortlisted for the Bridport and the Fish international short story prizes. She also received an honourable mention for the Lorian Hemingway short story competition. She has a BA in English, Sociology and Politics, and an MA in Modern and Contemporary Literature. She works in adult education and lives in Wexford south-east Ireland.

Anna Seidel
Anna Seidel is currently completing her MSt in Creative Writing at the University of Oxford alongside a career in economics. She previously read business economics and philosophy at the University of St. Gallen, Switzerland and at Harvard University. Also, she is the co-founder of the poetry foundation 'The Napkin Poetry Review'. Her poetic work has been published in Stanford University's Literature Journal Mantis, Stand, The Fiddlehead, Brittle Star, Inkwell, Marble Poetry, and Frontier Poetry, among others.

Clara Maccarini
Clara Maccarini grew up in the North of Italy. Here, she spent her teenage years discovering her passion for languages, before starting a journey that would take her across four continents, mixing study and work with an innate curiosity and longing to understand humanity in all its forms.

Denise O'Hagan

Denise O'Hagan is an award-winning editor and poet, born in Rome and based in Sydney. She has a background in commercial book publishing in the UK and Australia. In 2015, she set up her own imprint, Black Quill Press, through which she assists independent authors. Her poetry is published widely and has received numerous awards, most recently the Dalkey Poetry Prize 2020. https://denise-ohagan.com

Donka Kostadinova

Donka is an avid reader. Originally from Bulgaria, she immigrated to Ireland at the age of 25 and has been reading and writing in English since. An accountant during the day, a reader and a writer at night, she is currently pursuing an MA in Creative Writing from UCD Ireland. She writes short stories, essays and poetry. She lives in Dublin with her husband and two young daughters.

Ekaterina Crawford

Ekaterina Crawford was born and grew up in Moscow, and now lives in Aldershot with her husband and their two children. She always loved writing, but it's only in the past few years that she really pursued her passion. Ekaterina's creative pieces were published by the Visual Verse Anthology. *She has won Writers' Forum Magazine Poetry Competition and was placed 3rd in short stories Competition. She has also won the 2021 Kingston Libraries Short Stories Competition.*

Faith McNamara

Faith McNamara is a third year Scriptwriting student at Bournemouth University. Originally from Pitstone in Buckinghamshire, Faith has grown up surrounded by nature, and has drawn from her rural surroundings to create work centered on the themes of life and death. Faith has recently been focusing on her Irish heritage, exploring her family history and connecting with the culture. She's previously had work published by the Young Writers Group and continues to post her work online.

Fiona J. Mackintosh

Fiona J. Mackintosh (www.fionajmackintosh.com) is a Scottish-American writer living near Washington D.C. Her flash collection, The Yet Unknowing World, *was published by Ad Hoc Fiction in 2021. In 2018, she won the Fish, Bath, and Reflex flash fiction prizes and had work selected for Best Microfiction 2019, Best Small Fictions 2019, and the 2018-19 BIFFY 50. Her short stories have been listed for the Cairde Word, Colm Toíbín, Bristol, Galley Beggar, and Exeter Short Story Prizes.*

Helen Clark Jones

Helen was born in Yorkshire. After studying Fine Art in Brighton and a career as an Art Director in film and TV, she now lives on the South Coast where she achieved her ambition of planting her own seaside garden. She is currently engaged in mortal combat with the rabbits determined to destroy it. By day, she works in an art gallery overlooking the sea and by night, she writes short stories and fiction for adults and children.

Julie Evans

Julie Evans, from Guildford, took up writing four years ago. Her work has appeared in national and local newspapers, in anthologies, on local radio and audio, and she was a guest reader at the Guildford New Writers' Festival. She has won, been placed or shortlisted in many writing competitions. Judges have described her work as 'original and clever... bursting with colour and character.' Julie has a degree in History from Oxford University and a Creative Writing Masters.

Laila Lock

Leila Lock is currently studying for a Master's degree in Creative Writing at Bournemouth University. She lives with her family and an eclectic range of animals in Dorset.

Liz Houchin

Liz Houchin lives in Dublin. She holds an MA in Creative Writing from University College Dublin. 'Anatomy of a Honey girl,' her first chapbook was published in 2021. She was recently awarded a literature bursary from the Arts Council of Ireland. Her work has appeared in Banshee, Journal.ie, RTE, and has been shortlisted in competitions, including the Fish, Bridport, Irish Novel Fair and Fool for Poetry prizes.

Lucy Pearce

Lucy is a writer from the heart of Dorset who focusses on poetry and character-driven prose. Alongside doing a Masters in Creative Writing and Publishing at Bournemouth University, she is also writing her first novel and working as a copywriter. Lucy can often be found with a book in her hand and a cat on her lap.

Mary Byrne

Mary Byrne is a writer and artist. She has worked as an English teacher, a map archivist, a note-taker and an art tutor. She has had short stories published in magazines and anthologies. In 2019, Mary won the Leicester Writes Short Story Competition. She was shortlisted for the H.E. Bates Short Story Prize (2020) and 'Highly Commended' in the Frome Festival Short Story Competition (2021). She is currently writing more stories and a historical novel.

Maureen Cullen

Maureen writes poetry and short fiction. In 2016, she was published by Nine Arches Press, along with three other poets, in Primers 1. She won The Labello Prize for short fiction in 2014, and has stories published in Prole, the Hysteria Anthology, the Evesham Anthology, Leicester Writes Anthology, Stories for Homes Volume 2, Willesden Herald New Short Stories 10, Northwords Now, The Bristol Prize Anthology 2018, and online at Ink Tears, Creative Writing Ink and Impspired.

Milie Fiirgaard Rasmussen

Milie is a young woman fascinated by identity and culture. Having spent her teenage years in a small Danish town, she started searching for cultures to explore. As such, she now studies Creative Writing and

Publishing at Bournemouth University where she gets to fully explore her creative interests and develop her poetic skills. Her poetry often has the linguistic rhythms of a language nerd, and reflects personal emotions and memories.

Molly Smith Main

Molly Smith Main studied Drama and History of Art at university. As well as writing short stories and poetry, her passions are genealogy, history and preloved clothes, and painting and reading in her spare time. She completed her MA in Creative Writing and Publishing at Bournemouth University. She lives in a quirky old house stuffed with over 1,000 books and is happily married with two daughters.

Naomi Elster

Dr. Naomi Elster has a PhD in Science. Her stories have been published in Irish, American and International journals and anthologies, including Crannóg Magazine, Flight Writing, Meniscus, Geek Force Five, *and* Mosaics: An Anthology of Independent Women. *Her plays have been staged in Dublin, New York, and London. She is a former freelance science journalist with bylines including The Guardian, The Irish Times, Rewire and Proto. In 2020, she received the Tyrone Guthrie Award from Laois County Council to work on her first novel.*

Nina Cullinane

Nina Cullinane is a novelist and short fiction writer with an MA from UEA. She was recently shortlisted for the Bristol Short Story prize, appearing in the latest BSSP anthology. Her story 'Tulips' was editor's pick at Litro Online. She has written a literary novel about a twisted mother-daughter relationship set on the Isle of Wight, which has been placed in competitions by Arvon and the TLC, and is currently seeking representation from an agent.

Petra Lindnerova

Petra Lindnerova is based in South London. She works in the film industry by day and writes fiction by night. Her works have been previously

published by University of Cambridge, Fresher Press and Reflex Fiction.
She was shortlisted for the Fish Publishing Short Story Prize 2020/2021.

Ruth Wells

Rev. Ruth Wells is an ordained Priest in the Church of England, a mother, a University Chaplain, a justice-seeker and a creative agitator. She has a short poetry collection published by Proost entitled Formation and is an aspiring spoken word artist. Ruth believes poetry is magic and can unearth in us things which often lay buried and uncover within people stories which resonate beyond themselves.

Sharon Black

Sharon Black is from Glasgow and lives in a remote valley of the Cévennes mountains. Her poetry is published widely and has won many prizes. Her collections are To Know Bedrock *(Pindrop, 2011),* The Art of Egg *(Two Ravens, 2015; Pindrop, 2019), and a pamphlet,* Rib *(Wayleave, 2021). Her third and fourth full collections will appear in 2022 with Vagabond Voices and Drunk Muse Press respectively. www.sharonblack.co.uk*

Sophie Evans

Sophie Evans is a 22-year-old writer from Bournemouth, England. Growing up with a twin sister, her work often centres around the themes of sisterhood and family relationships. She has enjoyed writing fiction for most of her life, and sometimes dabbles in poetry.

Sue Finlay

After many years working as a Speech and Language Teacher, Sue decided to throw caution to the wind, and wave goodbye to the profession by enrolling on a Master's in Creative Writing at Oxford Brookes University, which she started in September 2021. She is fulfilling a long-held ambition to study English and creative writing. A new chapter has begun. Chapter one so far... But hopefully, there will be more chapters to follow.

About the Authors

Printed in Great Britain
by Amazon